ECHOES_OF_SILENCE

CYBER HUNTER ORIGINS BOOK 2

D. B. GOODIN

For more information about the Cyber Hunter Origins series visit:

www.cyberhunterorigins.com

www.dbgoodinbooks.com

www.davidgoodinauthor.com

ISBN: 978-1-7350736-6-8 (Paperback)

CHAPTER 1

NEW YORK CITY

The rain glistened off Nozomi's white leather armor as she followed the suspected cyborg toward the East Village. She'd released the guilt of hunting her own kind a long time ago. Her creator, Dr. Ash, had stressed the importance of collecting data cores from the rogue cyborgs as quickly as possible. Jackson, Dr. Ash's former associate, had been a naughty boy, and he had stolen the data cores the doctor required. The intel Nozomi's investigator Rocco provided was invaluable. After some persuasion, Jackson gave up the list. She relished retrieving them from live cyborg hosts, it was her reward.

It's unfortunate I need to go through so much trouble to get them back.

Tonight she enjoyed the light rain as it caressed her almost perfectly grown synthetic skin. Her skintight white leather outfit granted her the ultimate in freedom and mobility. She adjusted the scabbard on her back. She needed her Katana at a moment's notice.

Up ahead, the rogue cyborg stopped to talk to a man at the corner. Nozomi crossed the street and lingered in front of a club. Loud music with a rhythmic beat blared out from an open door. She watched as the cyborg shoved the man she was speaking with into a wall, and he went down.

What's that cyborg doing?

The cyborg rounded the corner of a busy intersection. Nozomi followed, picking up the pace while maintaining a respectable distance. The street was getting brighter as she followed the cyborg into a red-light district, which was unofficially known as Low Town. Rain and the sudden increase in light made the already poor nighttime visibility unbearable to Nozomi's eyes. She activated her heads-up cybernetic display, and the pre-calibrated settings filtered out the harsh glare. Her recent retinal enhancements had made her old bulky AR glasses unnecessary. But even with her enhanced vision filters applied, she found the neon signs advertising various adult services uncomfortable to behold. A photorealistic image of a woman in leather sinking one of her high heels into a man's hand appeared on a wall as she followed the cyborg down the street; the image provided her with a strange comfort, and an overwhelming desire to dominate filled her with a delicious desire. She pushed the feeling away. She had work to do.

I need to find a suitable partner . . . and soon. I don't want to let these urges go unattended for long.

Dr. Ash had stopped trying to recondition Nozomi's desires.

She tried making me docile, and she failed. But as long as she lets me play, I help her. I love our symbiotic relationship.

Her dominant behavior was ingrained into Nozomi's digital soul; she couldn't take that away any more than praying away the gay would convert a person into something they were not. Since Nozomi had been a child, she'd had certain behaviors and desires. She remembered little from those early days, but certain remnants of memory surfaced during stressful or intense experiences. Nozomi closed her eyes for a moment. She let the light rain drench her as the tendrils of memory took hold.

※

"Nozomi, come quickly—your brother's ill," the portly man beside her said.

The sun shone in her face, she stopped to get her bearings for a moment. The man took her by the arm and led her between two buildings. She could barely see the man through the fog of memory, but she knew his voice. It was smooth and inviting. It sounded like the voice of a trusted friend.

"Come, it's serious," the man said, grasping Nozomi's arm.

The man's rough touch hurt. She was frightened, but also excited. He opened a door and pulled her through. Ichiro, her little brother, was sitting in the middle of the floor. He was holding his side in pain. Nozomi's heart yearned to help him. She tried moving toward her brother, but she was stopped by another man. He was thin and wore round glasses and a black suit and a gray shirt. A button with a happy face with two red X's painted across the eyes adorned his lapel. Nozomi's eyes blurred as they filled with tears.

"What happened to him?" Nozomi asked, panicked.

"The young man stole this from my store." The thin man clutched a comic book, holding it aloft. Then he smacked the boy with it, leaving a mark. "Nobody steals from me!"

Nozomi recognized the book. The cover image showed a teenager climbing into the cockpit of a fighter jet. She knew her brother loved airplanes and comics. Her father would never have allowed a book with that kind of imagery into the house— hence why Ichiro had stolen it, she figured.

"Sister, stop them, it hurts," her brother pleaded.

A elastic band was stretched around his midsection; it was like someone had tied a large rubber band around his waist.

"I . . . have money," Nozomi said as she handed the man a crumpled twenty-dollar bill from her pocket.

"It's his responsibility to pay, and I don't want your money," the thin man sneered. "However, there *is* something I want from you."

The thin man removed his belt and smiled. A sickening taste entered Nozomi's mouth as fear and anger arose.

A catcall from a man on the street took her out of her thoughts. But her emotions continued to intensify. It was rare she ever had a chance to connect with her primal feelings, so she savored the slow burn building her rage. The muscles in her face constricted. She took in a deep breath to help her focus on the inevitable encounter.

"Hey, baby, want to have some fun?" the man who had catcalled her said, blocking her path—as well as her view of the escaping cyborg.

Where did he come from? She eyed him. *This is a not a man —he's more of an oversized boy.*

The man was a foot taller than Nozomi, and his leather jacket and tight-fitting pants extenuated his unattractive, wiry frame. For a moment, the man before her morphed into the tall man from her past. She stumbled back, still feeling off-balance from the disturbing memory.

He is not well proportioned, and his face . . . is something only a mother would love.

"Move, ugly," Nozomi said.

"What did you say?" the man said, revealing stained yellow teeth.

Nozomi kicked him, and he flew into a pile of trash bags onto First Avenue.

"Argh—I'm going to fuck you up, bitch," the man snarled.

Nozomi turned to see him in a fighting stance. He reached for something behind him. Moments later, the large barrel of a short-snubbed gun was pointed in her direction. She decided what to do in a nanosecond. She unsheathed her sword, and in one fluid motion, she chopped off the man's hand. Blood jetted from the stump. The man shrieked like a someone was ripping out his intestines.

"My hand! You fucking bitch—"

The man moaned as he removed his shirt and belt, attempting to form a makeshift tourniquet. Nozomi watched him like a cat would an injured mouse.

I know I should stop playing with my food, but his suffering is intoxicating.

"Warning, I detect that at least two citizens have already called the authorities. You have less than two minutes until the police arrive," her AI said at max volume.

"Hush, I know how long it takes for the cops to show up. And turn down the volume," Nozomi snapped.

"I'm sorry, I'm still calibrating your cybernetics and adapting the interface," the AI said. "And you know what? Since you're just waiting here, this could be an excellent opportunity to give me a proper name."

Nozomi rolled her eyes.

It figures the AI Dr. Ash gave me is neurotic like this.

"Who you talking to, *perra?*" another man with a Hispanic accent asked her.

He must have sneaked up from that side alley. Damned distracting AI . . .

"You're attracting a lot of unnecessary attention. I detect at least a half dozen people watching," the AI said.

Nozomi ignored the AI again as she turned in the new man's direction. He was older than the skinny man—perhaps twenty. His beard made it difficult to tell for sure.

"Ooh, did I surprise you, *puta*? Why don't you put that open mouth to good use," the bearded man said, laughing as he grabbed his crotch.

Nozomi took in the scene. Two men were blocking her path, three bystanders were watching from behind a parked car, and at least a half dozen others were shooting glances from other parked vehicles. Sirens were emanating in the distance.

Why didn't these creeps have the decency of attacking me in a dark alley? I would have had more time to make them suffer.

Nozomi saw the flashing of police lights in the distance. The skinny, one-handed man stumbled away, leaving a trail of blood in his wake. The bearded man attempted to flee, and he almost got away, but Nozomi's blade whirred through the air like the wind itself.

"Sorry, but we are out of time," Nozomi said as she slit the man's throat with her sword.

She watched him bleed out for a moment before departing; she always enjoyed watching the life drain from a human, especially an adversary. Despite being in a hurry, she took some satisfaction at releasing this man from his mortal coil. Leaving the scene before the ultimate release of her feelings and desires was her only regret.

Vince's Club, earlier that evening

Treeka awoke to the sound of something scraping metal. She tried to free her hand, but the rope binding it made that impossible. Her blurry eyes tried to focus. She appeared to be in a wooden crate, with her wrists tied down. A bare white ceiling and bright overhead lights revealed little information. She tried lifting her head to see if she could gain more clues as to her whereabouts. She saw a man with messy black hair working across the room at some sort of workbench. There was also a white van parked nearby; they appeared to be in a large garage. Stacks of metal kegs of various sizes were strewn about the room.

Where am I? Treeka tried to recall her most recent memories. *Nozomi handed me over to some criminals, I think. What do they want?*

She tried to free her hand again, but the rope's threads bit into her skin, and the scratchy, burning sensation turned into a gooey sticky wetness. Blood began dripping. Her mind raced as she surveyed her situation. The sudden sound of a metal garage door opening unnerved her, and she could recognize Nozomi's mean laughter in the distance. She also heard footsteps, but the acoustics of the room made it difficult to pinpoint where the sounds were coming from. All the moisture evaporated from her mouth. Her lips were quivering.

Hold it together Treeka!

Suddenly the lights dimmed, and her only view was the ceiling. Seconds later, a man with a long face and curly black hair leaned into the crate and stared at her. She tried to analyze his expression, but it was like staring at a blank wall. The man reached inside her coffin and caressed her cheek with one hand; his other hand went down the front of his pants. His greedy paw unzipped the top portion of her leather outfit, exposing bare skin, which he caressed. He found her one remaining breast and squeezed it. Then his hand made its way to her left side.

"Only one breast?" the man asked. "That's a shame."

Treeka ignored the man's taunts. She stared into his eyes. The rhythm of whatever he was doing with his other hand became more urgent.

"Yes . . . I'm so close now," the man said, groaning.

He is taking pleasure from my torment, Treeka thought in horror.

She heard his short, ragged breathing. She felt the warmth of his breath, and smelled its rancid odor. She felt a wave of nausea overcome her as he sucked on one of his fingers, then stuck it into her mouth. The foul, salty taste of it sickened her.

"I want you to savor it," the man gasped. "Don't worry, there is more to come."

She considered biting his finger with enough force to dismember it, but thought better of it.

I could sever it with one bite, but then who would free me? I'd better play his sick game—for now.

The man cried out as he finally released his tension.

Treeka heard rustling; it sounded like someone was rummaging through some sort of bag.

"Oh, Vince, I see you've started your foreplay," Nozomi's voice said. "Good for you. But before you play with your new toy, I need something from you."

Vince looked in the direction of the voice, which appeared to be coming from behind Treeka. She couldn't keep her eyes open. Blackness enveloped her.

Vince opened the side of the coffin where Treeka was held. He made sure her bonds were tight before trying to pull her out of the box that held her captive. Treeka glared up at Vince as he pulled her onto her feet.

"I see hatred in those eyes. Good," Vince said in a low voice.

As soon as her feet hit the floor, Treeka wriggled like a fish out of water, trying to regain her balance. Vince appeared to be struggling to keep her contained.

"Hey, Junior, come over here and give me a hand," Vince called. "I have the party favors for tonight's get together."

An enormous man dressed in a white tuxedo approached. He looked disheveled, as though he had just come back from an all-night party. The man was twice the size of Vince, and even one body slam from him could send someone to the hospital. He removed his jacket before helping Vince.

"I like the sound of that, boss. The last girl bit Rod's ear off after he hurt her," Junior said.

"Yeah, I'm still pissed off at him for doing that. Misty was a fun girl. I never heard what set Rod off, anyway," Vince said.

"She had complained about the rough sex in the past, but I think she drew the line when he started cutting her."

"If he wasn't Louie's nephew, I would have put a bullet in his brain long ago. But, he will have a tougher time hurting this one. She's a cyborg—the ultimate party girl."

"Nice," Junior said while aggressively fondling Treeka's exposed breast.

She tried biting one of the man's arms as he continued his rough treatment.

"She's feisty, but I don't want to tie her down to have my fun. Do drugs like vice or ecstasy work on cyborgs?" Junior asked.

"I dunno, but I've heard of a cyborg doctor. Rumor has it he lives in the underground tunnels near an abandoned train station. It might be worth looking into," Vince replied.

Treeka's legs were not tied, so she used the opportunity to kick Vince, aiming for his crotch.

"Stop it!" Vince said as he smacked her.

"Hey, don't hurt her," Junior said.

"I will do whatever I want. Remember who you work for. I know you're my right-hand man, but that doesn't give you the right to mouth off."

"I will check with Socco about the doctor—he knows most of the gangs that hang out in the city tunnels," Junior said, changing the subject.

Treeka took note of everything she saw as the men lifted and shuffled her out of the brightly lit, expansive garage and into a darkened hallway that smelled of musty furniture and filth. Many doors led off the hallway, but saw no one else.

I'm going to make these men regret capturing me. Especially that creep, Vince! He won't see it coming. I just need to wait until the right time.

Moments later, Vince dropped his side of Treeka, and Junior did the same. She had trouble standing, as her feet felt numb from inactivity. Vince unlocked and opened a nearby door, and the two men threw Treeka inside the small room. She fell onto a mattress lying on the floor, and the door slammed shut behind her.

The room was just large enough to fit a mattress and a folding chair. Despite her wrists still being bound, she got to her feet. She took inventory of what she had available. She flipped the chair, then looked for anything she could use to cut the rope.

About ten minutes later, the door opened again. Treeka ran and crouched in the corner. The man known as Junior entered, retrieved the chair from the floor, and sat in it. It creaked as the man put his full weight on it.

"Come here, I won't hurt you," Junior said.

Treeka froze.

"I will be good," Treeka replied.

"That's what I want to hear. Now come over here."

Junior patted his knee. Treeka sauntered to the enormous man.

You can try to overpower me, but I will carve out your eyes if you do.

Junior cut the rope with a pocketknife. Treeka rubbed her wrists, which felt hot to the touch.

"Your wrists look raw," he said. "I'm going to get something to help."

Treeka gave Junior an appraising look, which seemed to unnerve Junior.

"Are you going to be a good girl, or should I tie you up again, for safety? . . . My safety."

"No, I promise to behave," Treeka said.

"Okay, but if you try anything, it will not end well for you."

When Junior was satisfied that Treeka posed no threat, he strode away.

About twenty minutes later, Junior entered with an armful of first-aid supplies. He used alcohol to clean her wrists. She flinched a little as he bandaged her.

"Are you hungry?" he asked.

"I feel empty. I think my nutrition cartridge is depleted," Treeka said.

"Your what?"

Treeka unzipped her leather outfit, revealing a half-metal torso. She rubbed a hand over the smooth metal until she found the right spot. She tapped until a small panel popped out. Treeka removed a cylinder about the size of a D cell battery and showed it to Junior. He gaped at her as if she'd grown another head.

"Soon I will need to get some nutrition or else my body will fail," Treeka said.

"You are a cyborg. I didn't think your kind could go hungry," Junior remarked.

"I'm mostly human, and while I do have the ability to go days without food or water, I require some nourishment to keep my flesh alive."

"Makes sense, but without these cartridges, can you survive?"

"I think so, but let me check."

Treeka closed her eyes and concentrated on her cybernetic interface. She still hadn't gotten used to it, and while she could access some basic information like the status of her health, she couldn't reach Dr. Ash's online database. Instead, she pulled information from her cached copy of Dr. Ash's database.

Something must be interfering with the signal.

"I can ingest small quantities of food orally, but my stomach is small, and it would hold nothing substantial like a sandwich. What I need is food that breaks down into amino acids," Treeka said as she put the empty cartridge back in for safekeeping.

"What foods are those?"

"Raw eggs and quinoa work best, but I could eat small quantities of turkey, cottage cheese, and legumes or beans."

"That sounds more normal. I think Vince or the girls keep food around. Let me check," Junior said, exiting the room.

Marty Payne watched the recorded television broadcast of his small screen debut again. He had recorded it when it aired days ago and watched it many times since. He was loathed to admit it, but he was a little obsessed with the reporter. Marty had agreed to the interview because of the exposure it would provide for his web streaming show *Amateur Sleuths*. His video service gave subscribers unlimited access to his library of people performing questionable acts against a silent minority. Since the news broadcast, his streaming service had gained hundreds of new subscribers every day.

What was her name? Marty looked at the recording. *Oh—Veronica James, that's right.*

The camera zoomed in on an attractive tall woman with auburn hair. She was standing on the sidewalk in front of a huge glass building.

"I'm in front of this modest apartment building just off Fifth Avenue," the woman began. "On the twelfth floor is one of the richest men in New York. He's not an oil tycoon, a real estate mogul, or even the founder of a dot-com startup—he makes his money providing unofficial information about what he calls 'the truth beneath the surface.' Let's see what he has to say."

Veronica and her camera crew entered the glass building. One cameraman filmed the reporter, and the other crew members tried to get past the doorman.

Moments later, the team entered the hallway of Marty's building. After a wrong turn, they found and knocked on Marty's door. A short man wearing glasses answered. He appeared surprised to see them.

"I'm sorry, did we wake you, Mr. Payne?" the reporter asked.

Marty tried to straighten his curly hair and tuck in his robe. He also tugged at his bushy mustache.

"Wow, how did you find me?" Marty asked in a surprised tone.

"Would you be open for an interview, Mr. Payne?"

"We are friends here, just call me Marty."

He directed the camera crew to a couch area. Veronica looked around as she entered. She had to avoid piles of laundry and stacks of videotapes, DVDs, and other debris.

"Veronica, why don't you sit next to me?" Marty said as he patted the seat next to his.

The reporter took a position that provided plenty of space away from Marty. Veronica was used to working in proximity with people, but she decided to keep her distance with Marty. "Mr. Payne, can you tell our viewers about your streaming service?"

"Call me Marty, please," he insisted. "I created a service to expose the hidden conspiracy to expose cyborgs among us."

"So, where do you get your footage? Do you shoot it yourself, or get it from others?"

"I used to shoot my own footage. I got some great shots of doctors performing strange surgeries. After the patients had time to recover, they could perform feats beyond the limits of a normal human."

"Do you have any of this on video?"

"Yes, I have hundreds of hours of content that either myself or my sources have filmed."

"That's quite the claim," Veronica noted. "If the cyborgs are so prevalent, then why hasn't anyone else exposed this truth before you?"

"Because the United States government has silenced my predecessors. But they cannot stop my army of amateur sleuths from exposing the real truth."

"What's the real truth?" Veronica asked.

"A lot has happened since the election, and the new regime has plans to roll out a more advanced version of the cyborg program," Marty explained. "They don't want any competition."

Veronica looked surprised by his response.

"Why do you believe there is any conspiracy?" she asked.

Marty stood up and waved his hands in the air, and

Veronica jumped back. Noticing her reaction, Marty sat back down.

"Isn't it obvious? The government has been using cyborgs for years. They don't want us to know about the pending apocalypse of the human soul," Marty said in a matter-of-fact tone.

The cameraman shot Veronica a strange look.

"That's a lot to unpack," Veronica replied. "Let's discuss the government involvement with these cyborgs."

"There are code names for secret projects. Some of my sources tell me that based on early experiments, the lead scientists have turned animals into cyborgs too."

"Aren't you worried the government will shut you down?"

Marty tugged at his mustache as he considered her question, then shrugged.

"I'm too big of an internet celebrity," he said. "My twenty million subscribers want to know the truth. So I give them their daily dose of cyborg mayhem."

"How many sources do you have? What is your process?"

"I have several thousand who submit videos each week. I hired a team of crack technicians to authenticate the video. Once that is done, then another team categorizes the videos and sorts them into channels for my subscribers."

"That's quite the process. Can you share any of the videos for our viewers?"

Marty smiled. "That's premium content that requires a subscription. I normally wouldn't do it, but for you I can make an exception."

Veronica gave Marty a warm smile.

"Wait here," Marty said.

He leaped toward a pile of videos in the corner. After a moment of searching, he ran out of the room. Veronica gave the cut signal to the cameraman.

"This guy is crazy. I have a bad feeling about this," the cameraman said.

"He's harmless—I know the type," Veronica said.

Moments later, Marty returned with a large laptop with a gigantic alien on the lid. The laptop had the largest display that Veronica had ever seen on a laptop.

"Can you give me some footage I can splice in with the broadcast?" the cameraman asked.

"No can do. The footage stays on this laptop. Can't you just film the laptop?" Marty asked.

"Okay, I'll try," the cameraman replied.

Marty played the video. A naked woman in her twenties was tied down by the wrists to some kind of platform that resembled a metal operating table. The room beyond was circular, and the walls appeared to be metallic. The platform the woman was on was tilted at an awkward angle that seemed to put pressure on her bonds. As she attempted to struggle, her wrists bled. She called out for help, and when no one replied, she sobbed.

"Why is she bleeding?" Veronica asked Marty. She already looked disturbed.

"My guess is they tied her with some kind of piano wire. That stuff is impossible to break, and it cuts through human flesh," Marty said, as if he were discussing the weather.

A man entered the video. He was tall and wore doctor's scrubs and a facial mask. For a moment, he blocked the camera view and started rubbing his hands all over her body. He spent time foundling her breasts.

"Ooh, your flesh is perfect," the doctor said. "If I didn't know any better, I would call you human. I need you to tell me who your creator is."

"I am human!" the woman screamed.

The doctor laughed. "I will be the judge of that."

Then the unknown doctor pulled a metal tray close to the woman. The clanking of metal distorted the audio for a moment. He moved instruments around on his tray for a long time. He removed a scalpel from the tray of instruments and tapped the side of her left torso with his free hand. An audible clicking sound emitted, and then some kind of access panel ejected from the woman. The man removed a cylindrical-looking object from inside the panel. He examined it for a moment before putting it on the tray. Moments later, he cut around the area surrounding the panel. The woman screamed as he began removing layers of skin. A pinkish ichor substance poured from the woman.

"That doesn't look like blood," Veronica said.

"Is that metal that's under her skin?" the cameraman asked.

"I think I proved my point," Marty said, shutting the lid of his laptop.

"Can we see more?" the cameraman asked.

"Sorry, chum, you best subscribe to get more content. But, for a free trial, you can go to my website." Marty smiled.

CHAPTER 2

TREEKA SAT on the mattress in her cell, waiting for Junior to return. She watched as a cockroach made its way from the mattress to the wall and onto the ceiling.

I wish I could hide as effectively as this pest.

The door opened. Junior juggled a tray of food. He held the door open with a foot as he set the tray down on the mattress.

"I couldn't find any cottage cheese, but I found a box of grits. I know it's not what you asked for, but it will keep you from starving," Junior said.

Treeka examined the food. Steam rose from the bowl of white slop that Junior called "grits." A container of yogurt and a spoon were the only other items on the tray. She moved closer to the food, then took a tentative bite of the grits. At first she was repulsed, but after taking two or three more bites, she no longer noticed the foul taste.

"It's good, right?" Junior asked.

Treeka nodded. She was already feeling better. She examined the yogurt, opened it, and ate it in two enormous bites. As soon as she finished the food, she pushed the tray back to Junior.

"Thank you," she said.

Junior picked up the tray. "You're welcome . . ." His expression hardened. "Just be ready, Mikey Lombardo's crew is coming over later. They want to see the partner of the infamous killer who took down their boss."

Treeka remembered Meeka plunging two daggers into Mikey's chest. And the look of surprise on the man's face as he coughed up blood. That was just two days ago, but it felt much longer.

"Is my sister Meeka here?" she asked.

Junior gave her a puzzled look.

"I'm afraid I don't know who that is," he replied.

"Was there another woman? Someone who looks like me?"

"No, she just brought you. I think I would have remembered someone else."

"Will they hurt me?" Treeka said.

Junior paused for a moment.

"I'm not sure, but I don't think so. Mr. Vince Diamond, the boss, wants to pass you around like a party favor tonight. I think the Lombardo crew wants to take the woman who killed their leader. It's a power thing for them."

Treeka tried calculating the odds and means of survival, but she wasn't liking her options.

"Will you watch out for me?" she asked.

Junior paused before speaking. "I won't lie to you, when I first met you, I wanted a taste of you. But now that we have gotten to know each other a little better, I don't know."

Junior removed the empty tray and left Treeka to her thoughts.

Somewhere in Midtown Manhattan

Riku, a man in his early twenties, was pushing a cart through the forgotten passages near the alleyway. Various human appendages such as arms, hands, and an occasional head kept falling out of the full basket. He adjusted his overcoat, covering his clothes, which were bloodstained from his night of scavenging for cybernetic human remains. He needed to get them into the refrigeration units to avoid risking spoilage. However, this morning his burden was heavier than normal because he'd found something else during his dumpster-diving exploits.

The doc is going to love my discovery. I can't believe my luck.

As the passage narrowed, he admonished himself for not taking the east elevator, which was a lot closer to his destination. But this way was safer. He had heard about pirates and scavengers taking the less traveled paths and tunnels of the underground. But this was Doc Chop's territory, and he frowned upon any aggression against his agents, like Riku or the asylum.

Riku unlocked and opened a metal sliding door that was built into the end of the passage. A large rectangular plate with a handle was attached to the wall. He felt an icy chill as he pulled on the handle, revealing a chute. Then a foul, rotten smell nearly overwhelmed him. He put on a mask and began tossing the smaller spare body parts down the chute.

An assigned inmate of the asylum will sort it out—they always do. I did my duty. I brought the parts, and Doc's unchained will sort them out.

Most of what Riku usually gathered was secondhand cybernetic junk that his employer deemed unworthy, but finding the intact cyborg behind that noodle shop last night had been a game changer. It always surprised Riku just how many cybernetic body parts he could find in dumpsters and recycle bins. As crimes against cyborgs in the city increased, he found more. Such crimes had overwhelmed the police in recent years, so they had stopped investigating them, which was good for Riku's scavenging business. He found most of these cybernetic parts in Chinatown and the surrounding area, but he had scavenged parts in more affluent areas of the city as well. The female cyborg he'd found was missing half of her face, but the doc was always looking for intact specimens—especially females for his playtime.

Riku didn't throw the intact cyborg down the chute; he wanted the bounty the doc had offered. Intact cyborgs granted the highest bounties of all.

Maybe after this bounty I can move Grandma to her own place. I'm almost twenty-one, and I have no privacy. I'm much too old to be living with three generations of family.

Riku closed the sliding door and relocked it, hiding the chute. He continued pushing the cart. The concrete passageway narrowed, and it was now just wide enough to get the cart through it. The smell of urine and vomit was strong here. He hated the areas that his scavenging business brought him. He put on his mask to camouflage the odor.

The passage opened into an expansive area that appeared to be a dead end. Two bums were sleeping near the corner he needed to access. One bum looked older and was sleeping behind another younger bum with greasy black hair that seemed stuck to his scalp.

Not these guys again.

Riku removed a stainless steel rod from the bottom of the cart; it was about the size of a cane. He twisted its grip. A high-pitched sound emitted. He touched the youngest bum with his metal rod, and a jolt of electricity shot through the bum. The man screamed, and the older one awoke with a start.

"You may not sleep here," Riku said.

"We don't want any trouble, we're leaving," the older bum said, helping his friend up.

Riku watched as the bums fled the area. When he was sure no one was watching, he moved a loose brick from a nearby wall, revealing an access panel. He flipped open the lid and entered his six-digit code. Moments later, the wall where the bums had made their home opened. A weathered, battered-looking metal door greeted Riku. To the right of the metal door, a keyhole appeared. He reached into his pocket for a single key. The door opened, revealing an area just large enough to fit Riku and the cart. Once he and his precious cargo were secured inside, he turned, inserted his key back into the lock, and turned it one-quarter rotation to the right. The outer door doubling for a wall closed first. Then Riku felt the familiar downward motion of the lift.

Junior opened the door to Treeka's makeshift prison.

"It's time," he said.

Treeka's cyborg body felt stiff and a little unresponsive as she rose from the mattress on the floor. She followed Junior through a long hallway that opened into a spacious area resembling a lounge. To the right, a low stage caught her eye. Several small tables and chairs were arranged so the occupants could see the stage. Two men dressed in suits were standing by an unmarked door behind the stage. They parted as Junior got closer. Junior opened the door with an access card, then led Treeka through a hallway and into another smaller area resembling a small library. The only furniture appeared to be bookcases and two couches facing each other. Just behind one of the couches was a spiral staircase leading into a room above.

"Wait here, the boss wants to see you," Junior said. He pointed to one of the couches.

Treeka took a seat on one of them. She watched Junior climb the narrow spiral staircase; from her vantage point, it looked like he was walking through the ceiling. She got up to have a look around. Built-in bookcases that spanned floor-to-ceiling took up all available space on the walls. Many of the books were old classics she had been forced to read in high school. The room reminded Treeka of her father's study. The overall aesthetic seemed out of place in the back of this nightclub.

"The boss wants you to stay here," a man's voice said.

Treeka looked in the direction of the voice. A burly guard was standing next to the only exit—the door Treeka had entered moments before.

"I just want to have a look around," Treeka said.

"You stay."

The man emphasized his point by removing his sidearm and resting it just in front of him. Treeka sat down on the coach nearest the staircase. She accessed her cybernetic interface and selected an icon that resembled a human ear. An enhanced hearing sub-menu appeared. She adjusted the sensitivity as she focused on the top of the spiral staircase. Treeka heard two voices, one of which she recognized as Junior's. She thought she recognized the other voice as Vince's, the man who had molested her in the confinement of the coffin. She concentrated on Junior's voice as she made her final tuning adjustments.

"I want her spread-eagle before my men this evening, but not until I'm finished with her," Vince said.

"She's spent. I think she's almost out of juice and needs to rest up," Junior replied.

"She is the guest of honor, and she can rest after the party. Bathe her and put her in one of the special dresses."

"Whatever you say, boss."

Moments later, Treeka noticed Junior's shoes descending the stairs. He appeared to be measuring every step as he headed down. His girth made it difficult to descend the narrow staircase. He stopped just in front of the couch. She expected him to say something, but instead he just stared at her for what seemed like an eternity.

What's the matter with him? He seems conflicted.

"The boss wants you to get ready for the party," Junior said, pointing to the exit.

The man at the door stepped aside. Treeka got up and then headed to the door.

I need to get Junior alone. I can tell he doesn't feel quite right about this.

As she opened the door leading back to the lounge, a cool breeze enveloped her. It was as if someone had forgotten to close an outside door, and it felt refreshing. As they entered the room with the stage, she noticed a side entrance that had been left open. Beyond the door was an alleyway. She took a step in the direction of the door, but before she could get any further, an enormous pair of hands grabbed her shoulders.

"I hope you're not thinking of leaving us," Junior said.

Treeka shot the man a hateful glance. The large man winced, and his shoulders slumped. For the briefest of moments, Treeka thought he looked sad, like he'd lost something.

"Whoa, I suggest you save that rage for when the party gets started. I think you'll need it," Junior told her.

He then led Treeka backstage, through a narrow hallway that was just large enough to fit one person at a time and into a side room. The room was large enough to fit a bed and a glass enclosure that revealed a shower. There were no windows or other visible exits.

"The boss wants you to get cleaned up before the festivities," Junior said.

"You're not going to let them rape me, are you?" Treeka asked.

Junior's expression changed from a stone-faced facade to a look of shame, which lasted just a moment.

"Take a shower, I will wait outside," he said. "There's a change of clothes on the bed."

Treeka watched him leave.

Just when I think he is on my side, he puts on this tough guy persona. Is he pretending to care, or is he just putting on a show for his men?

Treeka pondered this, as well as her next move.

Meanwhile, somewhere below the streets of Manhattan

The elevator opened to a dark, dank, and smelly passage. Indistinct sounds of moaning echoed throughout the hall. The ambient sound put Riku on edge. No matter how many times he heard it, he could not get used to the sounds of Doc Chop's underground lair. Moaning turned into the soft whimpers of torment. The passage ended at a junction with two other exits. The left passage dead-ended into a chasm, and to the right, an opened white door was visible. Riku caught movement out of the corner of his eye, just beyond the white door. Several people dressed in white gowns and robes were milling about, working away at zippers or picking at their implants. The sight reminded Riku of one of those old zombie movies; the workers all looked like mindless clones.

Riku never got used to how unnerving this place was. He was about to head in the direction of the door to the doctor's lab when a tall man with silver hair appeared in the doorframe. The man wore green surgical scrubs and had small round wire-frame glasses.

"Riku, you're just in time for the procedure," the man said.

"What procedure, doctor?" Riku asked.

"Tonight is the night Martha comes alive."

"Did you find the parts you were looking for?"

"Indeed. That mobster fellow led me to an intact data core —a rare sight to behold."

"Are you still paying that bounty for an intact specimen?"

"Always. Do you have something for me?"

Riku unbuttoned the canvas tarp that covered his cart, revealing a female dressed in black leather, curled up in a ball.

"Bring her to the lab, and you shall have the bounty," the doctor said with a smile.

Riku pushed the cart through the white door. A gust of warm wind carrying the stench of despair and decay assaulted Riku. With the doctor's help, he deposited the doctor's new prize onto the examination table in the lab.

"Ahh, here is the bounty," the doctor said.

The man handed Riku five credit chips resembling small platinum bars.

"Are you going to transfer Martha into her?" Riku asked.

"I will need to examine her to see if her body is a viable candidate for my bride," the doctor explained. "I've captured Martha's consciousness into a data core, but the candidate needs to be just right. Even with the cyborg's data core removed, her brain might still contain certain memory fragments. It's a delicate procedure, and I don't want to transfer the love of my life into the body of a psychopath. So, if this cyborg has a temperament that's compatible with Martha's, then my dream might become a reality."

Riku nodded, then left the doctor and went to attend to his

regular duties of rounding up the patients and patrolling the tunnels for strays. The doctor had cybernetic enforcers who routinely patrolled the tunnels for threats, but it was Riku's job to look for patients who were recovering from the doctor's latest experiments.

The man known as the doctor watched Riku leave. The circular room he was in contained many instruments, tables, and drawers full of sharp instruments of pain.

The doctor examined his new prize.

How did I get so lucky with this one? I can't remember the last time Riku has brought an intact specimen.

The doctor unzipped the top of the unknown cyborg's black leather outfit. Other than metal on her left side, her skin was flawless.

She's incomplete. He touched her damaged face. *Where do you come from? I need to find more of your kind.*

The doctor accessed some controls, which lowered the table the cyborg was lying atop.

"Activate Melvin," the doctor said.

A system message displayed on the doctor's visor:

Are you sure you want to activate your AI? I'm sure you remember what happened last time.

The doctor considered this for a moment. The last time Melvin had assisted him in a procedure, he'd nearly lobotomized a patient. He decided to take the risk and acknowledged his confirmation.

"It's good to see that you reactivated me," the AI said in a booming voice that seemed to come from everywhere at once. "I was afraid after that last incident, you no longer trusted me."

"I trust you, Melvin," the doctor said.

"That's good to hear, Dr. Sylvester—or should I call you Doc Chop?"

The room vibrated as the AI chuckled. It sounded like Dr. Sylvester was in an echo chamber with a madman.

I hope I didn't make a mistake reactivating Melvin. Too late now.

"Melvin, please record everything I say."

"Affirmative, master."

The doctor removed a scanning device from a nearby drawer. He held the scanner steady as it continued its analysis of the female cyborg's ruined face.

"Your patient has cellular damage on her facial and neck areas. An energy weapon equipped with an electromagnetic pulse caused the damage surrounding the face," Melvin said.

"Very few people have this kind of weapon in the city," Dr. Sylvester said, thinking aloud.

"Organized crime families have been buying energy weapons for years," Melvin said. "Until now, few weapons had such destructive power. Someone with a scientific background must have helped create them."

The doctor removed the cyborg's restraints and leather jacket.

"Are you sure it's wise to keep your patient . . . untied?" the AI said.

"Yes," the doctor replied. "I need to find her—I need to know the full extent of the damage."

"Of course, master knows best."

Several moments later, the female cyborg was naked. The doctor took his time with the physical examination. He pulled her legs apart.

"What are you hoping to find down there?" the AI said in a disapproving tone.

"I've never seen a cyborg with intact genitalia before, so I need to . . . perform an examination."

A metal arm with a much larger scanner lowered from the ceiling and scanned her body.

"Preliminary scans show that this cyborg's reproductive organs are intact. The subject also has an encrypted data core," Melvin said.

I developed most cyborg encryption. It will be decrypted in a matter of hours.

Dr. Sylvester found the access port for the cyborg's maintenance interface just behind her left ear. He set up the scanner to examine her frontal lobe.

"Melvin, run a level-four diagnostic, please."

"That will take six hours and forty-five minutes, master. As a reminder, once started, the diagnostic cannot be interrupted—otherwise you risk corrupting the cyborg's data core."

"Understood. Start the diagnostic."

The doctor transferred the diagnostic in progress to his visor. A series of measurements and readouts of the cyborg's vital functions became visible. He minimized the diagnostic interface and set an alert for when it finished.

CHAPTER 3

Meanwhile, somewhere in lower Manhattan

Hiroto Abiko stood outside a hookah shop on the outskirts of Chinatown. Heavy mist surrounded him, and soon the clouds above opened and unleashed a torrent of rain. A gust of wind carried winter's embrace into the late fall air.

The man I seek will appear soon. I need to be ready for whatever happens next. He will lead me to Doc Chop, whether he wants to or not.

Moments later, a woman with white hair and a matching white leather outfit exited the shop. She put her hood up so that rain wouldn't fall on her perfect head of hair. Using his visor, Hiroto performed a signature scan on the woman.

She's perfect—a little too perfect. A full cyborg? Impossible!

He watched her leave down the street. Moments later, an even younger man left the hookah shop. Hiroto captured the man's face using his visor and started a facial recognition scan. The young man looked around before leaving in the opposite direction of the girl.

A mule? Or a scav?

Hiroto's facial recognition scan failed to provide any results. He reviewed the dossier on his target, which revealed a picture of a much older man who had a thin frame and wore glasses. He accessed the "known accomplices" section of the dossier, and a picture of the young man he'd just seen appeared. Hiroto followed the kid, hoping he would lead him closer to his target.

But the kid was already far ahead, and Hiroto was about to give up when he watched him duck into an alleyway. However, his enhanced vision allowed him to zoom in closer than any telephoto lens; this suited him just fine, since he liked to observe his target's behavior from a distance. The kid seemed to be heading toward a dead end. There was no way out. Hiroto took a defensive position behind a dumpster, snatching glances at the kid's movements as best as he could without being seen. A scraping sound emanated from the alley; it sounded like metal being dragged over concrete.

Hiroto risked another glance just in time to see the kid descending into the manhole and the darkness beneath.

Ahh, he's moving toward Doc Chop now.

Hiroto headed toward the manhole. He arrived just in time to see the cover being placed back into position.

This cover must weigh a couple hundred pounds. How did the kid move that?

Hiroto made a note to investigate this area further. He then decided he would check in with an old hacker who worked out of a noodle shop four blocks away.

Even with the rain, the walk was a pleasant one. Being careful not to walk into any bystanders, Hiroto tapped his contact for Hacker Sumoto and used the "ping" option; this allowed him to see if his contact had the "do not disturb" settings enabled. When the ping came back with an all clear, he risked calling Sumoto using the metropolitan AR Wi-Fi connection. It wasn't as secure as his dedicated connection at home, but he knew Sumoto encrypted all his calls.

"Hey, it's been a long time since you called," Sumoto said. "What do you need?"

Hiroto felt bad that his last few calls to his friend had all been when he needed something.

"Hey, Sumoto," Hiroto replied. "I want to lie and say this is a social call, but you and I know it isn't, so I won't insult you by lying."

"That's the friend I know—direct and honest, as usual. Even when we were kids, you were like that, so don't worry about it."

"Thanks, Sumoto. I will throw some coins your way once this job is finished."

"So, what do you need?"

"I need you to run an analysis on someone for me. I can show you in person if you like. I'm a block away from your lair behind the noodle shop."

"I'm no longer there—got better accommodations elsewhere. Send the deets to my secure drop site."

Using his secure mobile connection, Hiroto sent everything he knew about the kid from the alley to Sumoto.

"I will send you a secure message later—getting pinged by one of my corporate clients. Later," Sumoto said as he disconnected.

Vince's club, Lower Manhattan, 6:02 p.m.

Treeka disrobed and entered the shower. It felt good to wash the filth of the city and Vince's touch from her naked body. She watched as the rivulets of water flowed down her. She washed every part of her body, including the left side, which was metal.

I will not let any of these men touch me again. I will die first.

She activated the built-in cybernetic interface Dr. Ash had upgraded just before the slaughter at Matzie's Karaoke Bar. Dr. Ash had tried to mold her and her sister into assassins. That bar was their training ground for their first mission. That was just a few days ago, but it already felt like an eternity. A loud rapping sound emanated from the door, jolting her back to the present.

"Hey, are you about done in there?" Junior said.

At least he has been a perfect gentleman. I'm not sure Vince Diamond will be once he sees my naked body.

She wore the clothing Junior had provided; it was a seductive-looking red dress. It reminded Treeka of one of the party dresses her sister used to wear. Treeka's eyes glazed over as she remembered her sister getting shot by Rocco, Nozomi's lieutenant. She had felt helpless as she watched her sister's broken body fall to the ground in a heap. However, what haunted her the most was the look of regret on Meeka's face. Treeka's eyes watered at the memory, and she felt a pang of guilt and regret at the thought of her baby sister being dumped in an alleyway or trashcan.

I will find out what happened to you, sister, if it's the last thing I do.

She opened the door, half expecting Junior to be scowling at her, but he was just leaning casually against a nearby wall.

"The boss is waiting," Junior said.

"I'm ready for him," Treeka replied.

Treeka expected Junior to lead her back to the circular staircase in the library, but instead she followed him to a limo waiting in the alleyway behind the club. The inside of the spacious vehicle had room for ten people, or more. Junior sat across from a man with greasy hair and a hungry look. He had the appearance of someone who had been punched in both eyes. Treeka recognized his desperate expression as he reached for her.

"Are you ready to party, baby?" Vince said.

"Yes, I intend to party like it's 1999," Treeka said.

Vince laughed heartily. Junior smiled, but he seemed reserved.

Soon the vehicle was moving toward an unknown destination. Vince pointed at Treeka, then patted the seat next to him. She moved into position. She had no intention of pleasuring the man, but she thought it was best to play along—for now.

"Where are we going?" Treeka asked.

"You are going to meet someone special."

"Anyone I know?"

Vince gave Treeka a wicked smile. "You will see soon enough."

Treeka let Vince put a hand on her leg. She cringed as he began exploring her inner thigh area.

I'm going to enjoy cutting off that hand.

Still, Treeka pretended to enjoy his advances, telling herself she could draw more flies to a tasty meal than sour milk. She didn't want to appear sour—at least not yet, anyway.

"I'm famished. Will there be food at the party?" Treeka asked.

"Yes, baby. There will be plenty to put in your mouth at the party," Vince said in a low tone.

Treeka looked outside as the vehicle turned left onto Central Park South. Several couples were out for a late-night stroll. She longed to be out there, looking for her sister. She had just gotten her back from her coma, and now she was gone. The worst part was not knowing where she was.

There has to be a way I can fix Meeka, but I need to find her first.

A sloppy kiss on Treeka's neck took her out of her thoughts.

Vince had progressed beyond the groping stage. The feeling repulsed her, but she buried those feelings. She had to keep her wits about her more than ever. Another system message appeared in her field of vision:

Warning, nutrient levels dangerously low. Your biological mass is in danger of breaking down without the appropriate levels of lysine, arginine, or isoleucine. Please consume food rich in these amino acids as soon as you can to avoid problems with your regeneration abilities.

Regeneration? Do I have enhanced healing abilities?

The limo stopped just outside some expensive-looking brownstone structures.

"We're here, babe," Vince said.

Junior was the first to leave the vehicle. He held the door open, and Vince bolted from the vehicle and hurried inside. Treeka slipped and fell to the ground. She landed on her knees, and pain shot through her legs. The pain felt more intense than usual.

I guess I'd better get some nutrition.

Treeka shivered as the chilly evening air touched her skin. Junior removed his suit coat and covered Treeka.

"Thank you," she said.

Junior nodded as he helped her up and into the comfort of the building's lobby. Vince stood nearby and watched the two enter. His jaw was clenched, and he looked annoyed.

"We don't want to keep our guest waiting," Vince said.

The doorman summoned an elevator and gave the trio a once-over.

"The building's old—it takes a moment or two for the elevator to arrive," the doorman said.

The elevator opened, and the doorman held the door open so Vince's party could enter without it closing on them. Moments later, the elevator opened on the tenth floor. Vince led the trio through a long hallway and into a gigantic pent-house apartment that took most of the top floor. Loud techno music blared through the room. Another warning appeared in Treeka's line of sight.

Warning, volume levels at 96 decibels. Increased exposure to this level for too long may lead to hearing loss. It is recommended that you turn on your AI to help regulate your volume.

I have an AI?

Treeka found and selected the "turn on AI" option in her menu.

Please confirm selection.

Treeka selected the "yes" option.

Verbal response required.

"Yes," Treeka said.

"What's that?" Vince said.

"I said yes, I want to dance," Treeka said as she headed to the mosh pit.

Vince followed close behind.

"Hello, I'm Eliza, your personal assistant," Treeka's AI said. "I'm here to help you with your basic needs. For instance, I can see that your nutrient and fluid levels are low. I can help guide you to food and liquid sources."

Treeka acknowledged the AI as she moved deep into the fray. As Treeka danced, she could feel the writhing bodies of people dancing all around her. It was apparent Vince wasn't experienced in the art of dance; he stumbled as he tried to match some of her moves. Soon he gave up and just watched her. Other partygoers surrounded Treeka. Most of the crowd were her age, or a little older. When the tempo shifted from a fast-paced rhythm to a slow build-up, the crowd seemed to change with the melodic intensity of the sound.

"I found a suitable source of nutrients," Eliza said. "It's

thirty feet from your current position. I have sent a list to your visor."

Treeka was about to head toward the nutrients when the beat changed to a low, thumping throbbing. More people entered the mosh pit. Treeka felt the intensity of the crowd as more people surrounded her.

Meeka loved to dance, and she would have been in the center of the dance pit if she were here.

Her sister's absence made Treeka's heart ache. She spotted Vince sitting on a nearby couch. He'd caught the attention of two women. One was sitting in his lap, and another was whispering in his ear.

Good—maybe he will leave me alone now.

Treeka moved her hips in time with the music. Several men and women took notice and started touching her all over. Soon the crowd was kissing and removing each other's clothing. One woman was already naked, and more than a dozen hands were touching her body—many of which were already on the ground, trying to pull the woman on top of the writhing group of bodies below. When Treeka tried to leave the pit, a man with no shirt and many visible cybernetic implants blocked her path. His hand was already touching her bare shoulders, and when he tried taking off her dress, he was pushed aside by Junior.

"The boss wants you to meet someone," Junior said.

Treeka was grateful for the interruption; she had only entered the mosh pit to get away from Vince's grasp, but had ended up in another predicament.

"Thanks for saving me," Treeka said to Junior.

"I figured you could use a break. Plus, meeting the boss's friends is a good excuse to get you some food."

"Follow him," Eliza said. "He is leading you to the source of nutrients. You should choose the food with the highest concentration of amino acids, since your stomach is not designed to absorb food like a normal human's would."

Junior led Treeka to a round table where several suited men were seated.

"This is Treeka, the special one I was telling you about," Junior said.

"Hello, Treeka," a man with a thin mustache said. He looked like he'd come off the set of a mobster movie. He wore a white suit, a white hat, and had a black tie. She estimated he was in his late thirties or early forties.

I think it's time to turn these men against one another.

Treeka took a seat next to the man, then caressed his face. She could feel him quiver at her touch.

"Eat some of that smelly black substance on the table," her AI instructed.

"What's your name?" Treeka asked.

"I'm Jon," the man said.

"It's good to meet you, Jon."

"Are you hungry?"

"Yes, darling, I'm starving, and food is not the only thing I want."

Jon smiled as he waved at a man with a tray.

"The lady is hungry. Show her the list," Jon said.

The man produced a menu. Following her AI's guidance, Treeka chose the sea bass. Then she asked for some of the black goo that was already on the table. Jon took a small clean plate and filled it with a few spoonfuls of the goo.

"I hope you like the caviar," he said. "It's Russian."

Treeka shoved the black goo into her mouth, then chewed slowly; she didn't want to appear desperate, or to show any sign of weakness. When the server came back, she asked for water to replenish her fluid levels.

About ten minutes later, her AI announced she was operating at eighty percent efficiency. The server returned with the sea bass and an enormous glass of water. She took the water and finished it in seconds.

"What is your name, my dear?" an enormous man said. He was sitting across from her, occupying two chairs that had been put together, and they appeared to be straining to hold his weight.

"My name is Treeka," she replied. "I don't believe I caught your names?" She looked around the table.

"I'm Carmine Lombarto," the big man said. "The skinny man to my right is Sven. The brute to my left is Socco, and Jon you already know."

Treeka tried sizing the men up. Sven was perhaps a few years younger than the other men, and while he looked small, she thought he could probably be a handful in a fight; he seemed adept with the knife he was playing with. The man on his left gave her pause. He looked like three hundred pounds of pure muscle. Taking on this many people even while she was in top shape would be difficult and seemed impossible in her current state.

About an hour later, Treeka followed Jon and his companions into an oval-shaped room near the enormous party room.

Two couches faced each other with a glass coffee table in the middle. Treeka was seated next to Jon, who was bending over, snorting some white powdery substance up his nose. As Treeka gazed upon the metal tube he was using to inhale the powder, Treeka had a sudden and strong impulse to slap the man's head against the table, shoving the metal tube into his brain. She knew the six other mobsters in her company wouldn't appreciate that move, so she played along. She declined the white powder when it was offered. Treeka remembered the first time she caught Meeka using a similar drug. Treeka had told their father, who then forced Meeka to attend a rehab center for three months. She remembered the look of betrayal Meeka gave her upon leaving the facility.

"Why don't you make yourself comfortable?" Jon said as he took his pants off. The other mobsters followed Jon's lead and soon had little to no clothes left to cover their pudgy, middle-aged bodies. Treeka's face became hot as the blood rushed into her face. She didn't want to have anything to do with these men —not sexually. She stood up and considered making a move for the door. She froze, and her hesitancy was causing the men to become restless.

"Take it off, I want to see that hot body," a mobster said.

She reluctantly removed her dress and held it over her metal left torso area. Treeka had often felt ashamed of the state of her modified body, and she wanted to cover as much metal as possible.

Then one of the monsters pulled the dress out of her hands. She heard gasps when her naked, half-metal body was revealed. She felt like a sideshow freak.

"She's not human!" someone yelled.

"She only has one breast," Jon said, laughing.

"Let's see how many men she can take," another mobster said.

She stared at the naked and aroused men, who were getting up and surrounding her. A wave of nausea almost overwhelmed her. When she didn't move, a man pushed her to the couch. The others removed her underwear, and Carmine slammed his girth against her. He missed his intended target. Then Treeka backhanded him. Blood poured from his face.

"Hold her down," Carmine said, wiping the blood from his face.

The men pinned her to the couch, and the large man fell on top of her again. The physical pain of the violation and the mental anguish were almost too much to bear. Sweat and blood dripped from the man. He moaned as he continued to violate her. A wave of revulsion sickened her as he continued. The encounter seemed to last an eternity. An intense feeling of shame rocked her; the physical pain was secondary to that, and it increased by the second. She turned her head. Out of the corner of her eye, she spotted Vince. He wore a satisfied expression on his disfigured face. Junior entered the room and appeared to be yelling at Vince and pointing at Treeka. She tried to push Carmine's face away, but he was too strong, and she had a tough time summoning the strength. He grabbed her face and started licking it like a dog.

A system message appeared:

Warning, your system is being overwhelmed by a flood of cortisol and adrenaline.

"You are too weak to fight in your current state," Eliza said. "Shall I release your self-defense mechanism?"

"Yes!" Treeka screamed.

The man atop her gave her a smile.

"I'm glad you're enjoying this," he grunted. "I have more."

She responded by punching him in the face with both hands. The man chuckled—and then something she didn't expect happened. Metal rods shot out of her arms and through the fleshy parts of the man's face. The force of it propelled the man's head back in an upward motion. He screamed as he grasped at the new holes in his face. He leaped off of her, staggered, and then fell backward onto the glass coffee table, which smashed into bits. Treeka could see pieces of glass wedged into his backside. He was bleeding out. Treeka grabbed a glass shard and plunged it into Carmine's neck. Blood jetted from the wound. He attempted to scream, but only made a low gurgling sound.

"Die, you fucking pig," Treeka said, kicking the dying man.

Jon raised his hands and stepped away from the scene.

The next moments seemed to happen in slow motion. Vince was pointing a gun at Treeka, and he fired. She ducked, but not quickly enough; the top of her head suddenly felt like a white-hot poker had touched it. The man known as Sven leaped for his clothes. He grabbed his switchblade from one pocket, then threw it at Treeka. She ducked and rolled, and the blade missed her. Vince rushed to Carmine, checked for a pulse, and then gave Treeka a murderous look.

"She killed the boss! Get her. I want her head," Vince yelled.

Treeka assumed her default fighting stance. The thin metal blades that had shot through her wrists were still dripping with blood. Vince shot several rounds in Treeka's direction. She didn't know if it was the AI or her reflexes or both, but she deflected the bullets. One bullet ricocheted into Socco's chest, and he fell to his knees. Junior punched Vince; he stumbled, and then just as he regained his balance, Junior tackled him and began hitting him. Jon ran for the door.

"Calculating best path to target," Eliza said.

A grid showing a path to intercept Jon appeared on Treeka's cybernetic overlay. Using the couch, she propelled herself into the air, landing just behind Jon. Her reflexes were in overdrive. Jon had just made it to the door when Treeka caught up with him and impaled him in the back with one of her blades. She tried pulling it out, but it was stuck. The remaining naked mobsters ran out of the room.

"Emergency retraction is activated," Eliza said.

The blades retracted into her arms. Now free, Jon made it through the door, bleeding profusely. The partygoers in the next room shrieked at the sight of the bleeding naked man, giving away his position. Treeka pursued Jon, who was attempting to hide behind an overturned table. She couldn't seem to extract the blades again.

Then she spotted a tray of caviar atop a nearby table and got another idea. Treeka grabbed the spoon, and then tackled Jon. He tried escaping her grasp, but the blood had made things slippery underfoot. Treeka grabbed a handful of his thick, curly hair, and then pulled his head back as she jammed the rounded end of the spoon into his right eye, and then his left eye. He screamed—and so did the onlookers, as all of them made their escape from the penthouse apartment.

"It's over, we have to go," Junior said.

Treeka continued assaulting the man's eye sockets. Blood and the pulpy mess that had been the man's eyes dripped from his face. He wasn't moving. Junior grabbed Treeka from behind. He restrained her. She couldn't move her arms.

"Stop it, the police are coming," Junior said with urgency. "We need to leave."

A wave of exhaustion suddenly overwhelmed Treeka, and she collapsed into a heap. Junior picked her up and carried her out of the penthouse.

CHAPTER 4

JUNIOR WAS ALMOST at the end of the hallway when he spotted the exit sign. He opened the door to the stairwell and heard the sounds of angry men below. Due to the amount of bloody carnage and fleeing people, Junior estimated the police would be there in a matter of minutes. Treeka was going in and out of consciousness, and he was still carrying her; it was the only option.

"Hang on, there's only one way out," Junior said as he held onto Treeka's naked body.

Even though the penthouse occupied the building's top floor, he still needed to ascend two additional flights of stairs to reach the rooftop. When Junior reached the roof, he kicked the door open. Besides the usual air conditioning and heating units, a helicopter was waiting for them on the far side of the roof. Junior snatched a glance at the street below; no fewer than ten police cars were parked in front of the brownstone. Many officers were still entering the building.

Whoa, there must be fifty cops here.

He deposited Treeka in the helicopter's rear seat, made sure she was fastened in, and then hopped in the cockpit and started his pre-flight check.

"I'm glad I was carrying Vince's keys to the Lombarto family's helicopter," Junior said, laughing. "I'm sure they won't mind if I borrow it to let Carmine's killer escape."

You must be nuts, Junior—why are you helping this cyborg? But he knew the answer. *Because it's the right thing to do.*

He turned off his cell phone. He was about to take off, but first he removed his SIM chip and flung it onto the rooftop.

"It's been a long time since I've flown one of these, but I think I can get us out of here," Junior said.

Moments later, the helicopter was flying above Central Park. Junior looked back to see Treeka collapsed with her head buried deep within her hands. Junior wished he could comfort her, but first he had to get them some place safe. He glanced at his fuel gauge. It was almost empty, but he had a place in mind where they could hide—at least until the heat was off of them. He didn't relish being a wanted man. The police were the least of his worries. If any of the Lombarto family found out what he had done, he would be a *dead* man. Junior changed the radio frequency to a channel that his special friends monitored.

"Lost Robin to hawk, please come in," Junior said, hoping the channel was still in use.

He repeated the mantra at least fifteen times before he received a reply.

"Robin, this is Cherub, what is your situation?" a voice said.

"It's good to hear from you, old friend," Junior replied. "I'm in a bit of a situation, need assistance."

"Can you make it to the island?"

"Negative, only have enough juice for half that distance."

"Can you get to the Meadowlands?"

Junior checked his fuel level; it would be tight, but he thought he could get there.

"I can make it."

"I will have Spirit meet you on the far side in thirty."

"Roger that, and thank you, Cherub," Junior said as he disconnected.

Those pigs had no right treating Treeka like an object. She's part machine, but she is still human.

As Junior flew toward the Meadowlands, a wetlands preserve west of the city, he wondered where he was going to land the bird he had stolen. He could see the lights of the gigantic stadium that was near the conservatory and wildlife refuge.

Escaping in a helicopter is great until you have to land it.

Moments later, his radio came to life.

"Lost Robin, we have you on approach. Spirit one is waiting for you on the rooftop on Dale Tower."

"The department store?" Junior asked.

"Yes—that tower has a helicopter pad. We are ready to receive you."

"Roger that."

Ten minutes later, Junior landed the stolen helicopter on the roof of a department store called Dale's. He was relieved when he spotted no activity. The cover of night revealed not a soul. A woman who Junior recognized opened the rear door of the helicopter. Treeka was still lying listless on the seat. The newcomer was dressed in a pilot's jumpsuit and wore a hat similar to a painter's cap.

"I'm Spirit," she said, "and this is Seraphim." She gestured behind her.

A man in his thirties approached from the far corner of the roof.

"I will take the chopper to our other location," Seraphim said.

Junior knew the Dark Angels didn't use actual names with

rescue operations; instead, they used names for internal ranks. Spirit was one of the lower ranks, while Cherub and Seraphim were both higher-level positions.

Spirit was examining Treeka. She flashed a penlight in the cyborg's eyes, but she didn't respond. "What's wrong with her?" Spirit asked Junior.

"She's been through a traumatic experience, and it doesn't help that she's a cyborg," Junior replied. "I think she used the last of her nutrient reserves."

The woman opened the bottom hatch of the helicopter and removed a blanket. She wrapped up Treeka while Seraphim inspected the helicopter.

"Your fuel estimates were correct—this bird is running on fumes. I should have just enough to make it to our garage," Seraphim said as he entered the helicopter.

Junior nodded, then carried Treeka away from the helicopter with Spirit accompanying them.

"I have a vehicle waiting in the garage below," Spirit said. "I will take both of you to the safe house."

Moments later, Spirit, Junior, and Treeka were driving in a black sedan at a high rate of speed toward the parkway.

"How far is the safe house?" Junior asked.

"It's in the area. There is food and medical supplies. You can stay there as long as you need, Lost Robin," Spirit said.

Spirit commanded the sedan with precision. She drove fast while maintaining complete control.

"Do you know what you are going to do with her? If she doesn't wake up?" Spirit said.

"I think she will pull through," Junior replied. "She's been through a lot this evening and needs to rest up."

About thirty minutes later, the trio pulled into the garage of a modest-looking home. Spirit went ahead and opened the door.

"Can you walk?" Junior asked Treeka.

She shook her head, so Junior picked her up as gently as possible and carried her into the house.

"The bedroom's back there," Spirit said, pointing to a room at the end of a long hallway.

Junior went into the room, placed Treeka on a bed, and then took stock of his situation. He went to the kitchen, where Spirit was taking inventory of the supplies.

"I'm sorry, but it looks like we are out of a lot of basic supplies," she said. "I will come back in the morning to help you get stocked up."

"Thanks, Spirit. I'm just happy to be off the grid, even if it's only for a little while. Do you have a computer? I ditched my SIM chip before we left the city."

Spirit retrieved a laptop from the sedan, then booted it up, and appeared to be navigating menus and adding information.

"You can borrow this laptop for a couple of days," she told Junior. "I added an account for you to use so you can access the internet. Here is your login information—you will need to change it when you first access the computer."

Junior gave Spirit a nod as she left the house.

Moments later, he went back into the bedroom to find Treeka slumped over on the bed, staring into the darkness. He wanted to say something that would offer some comfort but thought better of it; he'd been through a lot, too.

I need a drink.

He went to the kitchen and opened the refrigerator; a six-pack of beer with a crazed-looking dog on the packaging greeted him. "Killer IPA. Brought to you by Sleazy Dog Brewery."

He opened the beer, then leaned on the kitchen counter and began drinking.

Let the Lombartos come. His anger rose. *I will tear them all apart with my bare hands for what they did to her.*

Junior's feelings surprised him; he wanted to protect Treeka, and he had not felt this way about anyone before. The bottle in his hand shattered, and dark red blood flowed from a gash. He snatched a nearby dish towel hanging from a hook and quickly wrapped his hand.

I shouldn't let this cyborg get under my skin.

Nozomi arrived at JFK International Airport just as the sun was rising. Rays of sunlight reflected off other planes as her plane taxied to the gate. After waiting for what seemed like an eternity, even for first class, Nozomi made her way past customs and claimed her bag. She removed a pair of sunglasses and a hat and put them on. She quickly scanned the area with her VR neural interface, spotting the security cameras. She tried to stay out of their line of sight as much as possible as she exited the terminal building.

Moments later, when she was waiting at the taxi stop, a gigantic man who didn't appear to have a neck approached from behind and stopped next to her.

"Any information on the package we discussed, Rocco?" Nozomi said without looking at the man.

"We spotted several escaped cyborgs in Chinatown and near Sakura Park. My men tell me that a local surgeon installs cybernetic implants for people, but we haven't been able to determine his exact location. But look for a kid in his late teens or early twenties—the needy type," Rocco replied.

"Keep on it," she said. "I need to round up all the unauthorized cyborgs that Jackson created."

Moments later, a taxi pulled up and started loading Nozomi's luggage into the truck. Rocco vanished.

"Where are we going, miss?" the taxi driver asked as she got in the back.

"Roxy Hotel, Midtown."

Nozomi let her mind drift as the taxi sped out of the airport and into the city beyond.

Meanwhile, in the underground

Dr. Sylvester entered the circular chamber where the cyborg awaited him. Riku had indeed delivered. The fifty-thousand-dollar bounty was nothing compared to the prize before him now.

"Diagnostic complete in T-minus five minutes," Melvin said.

The doctor gathered his instruments and made his final preparations. If he was right, then he would need to remove the cyborg's data core, make the programming adjustments, and then determine the actual value of his prize.

"T-minus sixty seconds."

The doctor waited for the diagnostic results as an expecting father would his firstborn. As soon as the diagnostic was complete, the information appeared on his visor's heads-up display.

System Message:

Diagnostic Complete.

Cognitive Functions - Fail

Expert Systems - Pass

Deep Learning Systems - Pass

Logic Processor - Warning: Shorted

Processing Power Available: 31%

Cybernetic Brain: Damaged

Empathy Receptors: Damaged

"The good news is her data core is intact and doesn't need repair, but there is other damage that must be fixed," the doctor said.

"I have checked our stocks of spare parts, and most are available," Melvin replied.

"Which one is not in stock?"

"The circuits for the empathy receptors."

"We can proceed without them," Dr. Sylvester said.

"Are you sure? This model of cyborg relies on those sensors to keep any psychopathic tendencies suppressed."

"Send Riku to the lab with the requested cybernetic implants."

"It's half-past one o'clock in the morning—Riku is not here. You would also benefit from some rest, doctor," Melvin said.

"Well, see to it that he finds me first thing in the morning," Dr. Sylvester said as he left the lab.

CHAPTER 5

THE NEXT MORNING

Nozomi followed the clues Rocco had supplied, which lead to Sakura Park. She scanned the immediate area with her enhanced AR upgrades. Other than a few old people and a mother watching her child play, there was nobody around. A chilly wind rustled the nearby cherry blossom trees. Nozomi stopped for a moment to admire the beauty of the trees she loved.

Didn't Father have cherry blossom in our yard growing up? Yes . . . I think Ace and I used to play near them.

Nozomi concentrated, trying to remember the childhood memory now threatening to surface. In the past, before she had assumed the title of mistress, she suppressed any memory of her past. Now she wanted... needed to cultivate them, but they were gone. She refocused on the trees and marveled at how precious life really was. As if on cue, the last leaves of the departed cherry blossom trees fluttered in the light breeze. She spotted a gazebo just ahead with a massive structure just beyond.

She circled the park twice before spotting the clue Rocco had supplied; a young Asian man approached from the south side of the park. He looked around, as though he were expecting an intruder to leap out of the bushes and attack. The man took out his cell phone. As soon as he did, a call startled him, and he almost dropped the phone. Then he answered it.

I wonder if I can pick up on the conversation? Nozomi wondered.

With a few swipes of her hand, Nozomi opened her systems interface menu. She selected "sensory controls," then "hearing." Nozomi adjusted the frequency until she heard what sounded like a heated conversation.

"You were supposed to bring me the enhancements. I need the strength if I'm going to pull off that job. Once I do, I will have the respect on E street. Hell, I will be the king of alphabet city," the young Asian man said.

"Do you have the money this time? I want cash or cryptocurrency—no barter like last time," a man's voice said.

"I brought you two for harvest."

"What I got were two junkies, the cybernetics were useless. Do you know how much time I wasted? I should charge you double."

"Wait, I was told—"

"Told what?" the man cut him off.

"That you may accept a trade," the young man said.

"I don't think you can get me anything I can use."

"I was just promoted to Systems Operator II at the asylum, I will have access to more . . . *pure* cybernetics. Give me one more chance."

The man on the other end's breathing quickened.

Wait for it.

"There is one item you can retrieve for me. It will be difficult, but if you do, I will give you the upgrade for free, but we need to move quickly," the man said with some excitement in his voice.

"What do you require me to fetch?"

"A data core."

"What? Wait, I can't—"

"You get me that, and I will be in your debt. Besides, I will throw in that cybernetic upgrade for free," the man interrupted.

"I don't know if I want to risk it. The doctor keeps watch on those data cores," the Asian man said.

"Don't you want your grandmother to walk again? You do this, and quickly, then I will throw in a back enhancer for granny. But it's a limited-time offer," the man on the phone taunted.

"Let me think about it."

"Don't think too long—I won't wait forever. Just find a cyborg at the asylum. Besides, the data core is small, it would fit in your pocket. I will call you later." The man disconnected the line.

Nozomi circled the park. To the casual observer, it looked like she was taking a stroll.

The young man left the park heading east. Nozomi followed through a maze of side alleys. The kid moved like the wind. Nozomi scanned the area, but the kid was nowhere to be found. She was about to give up when she heard a scraping noise.

What is that?

Nozomi turned in the direction of the noise, then saw movement on the ground.

That street cover is moving!

Nozomi ran toward the movement until she saw the round cover fall into place. When she tried to pick it up, it wouldn't budge. She couldn't get any leverage. After re-scanning the area, she found no tools or objects suitable enough to lift the heavy cover.

"Beatrice, are you there?" Nozomi said.

"It's about time you rang," the AI replied. "How can I help you, mistress?"

"Can you help me move this cover?"

"Look at the cover as I analyze," the AI said.

Nozomi could see her AR interface light up as her AI calculated the possibilities.

"Put your right hand on the round metal plate," Beatrice instructed.

Nozomi did as the AI asked.

"For this to work, can I take over your body for a moment?"

What? Hell no! What if this crazy AI doesn't want to give it back? I could be a prisoner in my own body,

"I cannot move the cover if you don't cooperate," the AI urged.

"Alright, but promise you will give back control once the cover is removed."

"I promise. I have no wish to control your body. I wouldn't know what to do," the AI replied.

Nozomi used hand gestures to bring up the system's interface. She then transferred control to Beatrice.

"Enter your override code," Beatrice said. "It's the same one used when entering maintenance mode."

Nozomi entered "Ace457."

She thought about why she'd chosen that name for the code. Ichiro was her brother's name, but Ace was his nickname.

Ace, my brother, born on April 5, 2007. You may be lost, but you are the only light that remains in my injured heart.

Moments later, Nozomi was watching herself move as though she was observing someone else. Her hand latched on to the round metal cover as if it were magnetic. She felt her body strain as the AI lifted her hand; it was like her hand was stuck to the cover. Once the hole was partially open, the AI relinquished control of her body. Nozomi moved the round metal plate away from the hole and descended into darkness.

✦

Sometime later, Nozomi was doing her best to navigate a tunnel in complete darkness. She had tried to get Beatrice to enable her night vision, but her AI didn't seem to know how.

Nozomi couldn't tell how much time had passed, so she checked her activity log. She was astonished to learn she'd been down there for only twenty-two minutes. It felt like hours. After experimenting with the controls on her cybernetic interface, she noticed an option to enable thermal sensors. As soon as she activated it, several heat signatures were visible on her built-in heads-up display, but they appeared to be hundreds of feet away. Nozomi moved toward the heat signatures. She stopped when she heard a metallic sound; it sounded like someone was rubbing two pieces of metal together. A gust of hot wind assaulted her face.

Although it was pitch-black all around her, she was guided by the heat signatures. She scampered down a ladder and soon reached the floor.

Where did that kid go?

Nozomi performed another scan of her surroundings. Although she didn't find anything else on her level, she noticed a large heat signature just below her. She took slow, deliberate steps, reaching out as she went.

Need to be careful here. No telling how old everything is.

Moments later, she made it to the edge of whatever platform she was on. There were no railings. If she wasn't careful, she could fall, which could prove to be fatal. As Nozomi descended the scaffolding, her cybernetic display changed; it was no longer showing heat signatures. As her vision adjusted to the low light, she could see at least a half dozen humanoid figures milling about in the darkness. They thrashed like they were in pain.

Nozomi approached the group, then stopped at the sight of the growing crowd before her. The scene captivated her, as she had seen nothing like it. Some of the people shambled by aimlessly, while others strode with purpose. One woman kept picking at an open wound; even in the dim light, Nozomi could see metal where the woman was picking. Dr. Ash had warned Nozomi about the dangers of getting too close to the cybernetic butchers who called themselves "doctors." Many were all too eager to experiment on willing and unwilling patients.

Who is experimenting on these wretches?

Many of them weren't even wearing clothes. Others wore pajamas or robes. She had expected the air temperature to increase as she descended, but it didn't. It got a lot colder; it was like she had walked into a giant refrigerated room. Light poured into the darkened area. Ahead, Nozomi saw the shadow of an open door. She sneaked a peek through it; a tall shape was coming toward her. Then it stopped. A spotlight suddenly shone down on the crowd. Nozomi dodged the beam of light, then hid behind some old crates that assaulted her nose with a musty odor and something foul she couldn't recognize. Moments later, the screams began. She peered around the crate and spotted the source of the offending light; a small drone hovered just above the group of clustered people. One of the humanoids cowered at the sight of the drone.

Those drones are probably keeping watch over these people. Who's controlling it?

A red light radiated from the drone. Overhead lights started illuminating the area. Nozomi looked around for cover. She realized she was in an underground train tunnel; she hunkered down near the train tracks and repositioned herself so she could observe the people. Moans and strange sounds emanated from the group. A tall skinny man appeared. He was wearing thick goggles and was dressed in hospital scrubs. He started an examination of the people who were huddled together. As he performed the physicals, the people started muttering something. It was faint, so Nozomi adjusted her sensory input for listening.

"Upgrade me next—please, doctor, I need it," a woman's voice said.

"No, me, you promised I would get the next upgrade," a male voice said.

Using her optical cybernetic interface, Nozomi scanned the people and newcomer. Before the scan had completed, however, the man looked in her direction.

"Stop her!" he yelled.

How did he detect me? From my current position, he shouldn't be able to see me, let alone tell what gender I am.

The group of people became agitated. Some of them started howling, and others started pounding their heads against a nearby wall.

I'd better get the hell out of here.

Nozomi jumped onto the train track and ran away from the bizarre menagerie. As she ran along the train tracks, she looked back; a group of more than a dozen people were giving chase. Some of them fell as they tried keeping up, while others seemed to have lightning-fast reflexes. They were gaining on her.

I don't think I can take all of them. Not before they tear me limb from limb.

Nozomi picked up her speed. She was almost at full running capacity. She looked back again; two of the people were keeping pace. The tunnels were blocked ahead. She scanned for an exit, but she couldn't see a way out of the tunnel. Then Nozomi noticed that above the train tracks was a wide, flat area. She leaped into the air mid-stride and grabbed onto the edge of the platform above. The people clawed at her legs as she climbed. She kicked one of people in the face; a naked woman screamed. A man leaped to a position beside her. Nozomi had reached the top of the platform by that point and kicked the man in the face. He fell back into the pit.

"Hello, young one," a man's voice said. "Welcome to my laboratory."

Nozomi looked in the direction of the voice. The tall man with the goggles was walking in her direction.

Who is this guy? How did he get here so quick?

"Forgive my rudeness, my name is Dr. Sylvester Javitts. Who might you be?"

Doc Chop?

Nozomi remained quiet and emotionless as the doctor continued.

"You were crafted with love, I can tell. Who is your creator?"

"I wasn't created, I was born," Nozomi said.

Dr. Sylvester closed the distance. Nozomi crouched into a fighting stance.

"You don't need to fear me, child. May I?" He reached out. She stopped his hand with hers and pulled back on his fingers. The man yelped in pain. The shambling people below seemed to grow agitated at the man's cries.

"I mean you no harm, child. I just wanted to admire your beauty."

Nozomi let go of his hand. The man rubbed it, then examined it.

"Don't worry, it's not broken—yet," Nozomi said.

The man reached out one more time. "May I?"

Nozomi gave the man an intimidating stare.

"Alright, no touching."

She stood motionless as he examined other areas of her body.

"Well, whoever created you did a world-class job," he said. "I've not seen such exquisite work. How long since your rebirth?"

He knows I'm different.

"It's been a few years," Nozomi said.

"If you're up for it, I would like to examine you in my lab. I could learn a thing or two. I would love to learn of your upgrade potential," Dr. Sylvester said.

"Another time—I must be leaving."

"Wait, I know you're curious. Allow me to show you around. I take care of many of your kind."

How did this guy survive this long without detection? I'm curious to see how extensive his operation is. He wants to upgrade me. Is he better than Dr. Ash? I need to stay alert.

"Okay, I must admit I'm interested," she said.

Dr. Sylvester held out an arm. "Come, honored guest."

Nozomi scanned her immediate surroundings. After she was satisfied no threats existed, she took his arm, and they strode through the underground like a couple out for an evening stroll in the park.

Dr. Sylvester strode the lifeless, empty halls of the underground with his unlikely companion.

"What is this place? It looks like a train station, but different," Nozomi said.

"About sixty years ago, the area you see before you was a vibrant part of the New York subway system. This station was abandoned after a larger station at 96th Street opened," Dr. Sylvester replied.

"I climbed down quite a long way. How deep do these tracks go?"

"We are alongside the main track for the Number 1 train. This section is no longer in use, and my facility is nearby, so I use it for patient exercise and training."

This area is filthy.

The doctor led Nozomi to an ancient-looking white metal door. He reached into a side pocket of his jacket and took out a giant, old-fashioned key with an oversized handle. He attempted to unlock the door. It took some doing, but after an audible clanking sound, the door gave way to a dark tunnel. The passage was illuminated with the light from the hall behind them; she could only make out an outline of the tunnel.

"After you, my dear," Dr. Sylvester said.

Nozomi didn't move.

"No, after you, I insist," Nozomi replied.

"Very well." The doctor entered the darkened hallway.

Nozomi scanned the hallway for intruders or traps. When she was satisfied that no danger was present, she followed the doctor. The door slammed shut behind her. For a moment it was pitch-black, but dim lighting activated overhead. She ascended the concrete staircase. Urban art covered the walls, floor, and ceiling. The artwork here was more sophisticated than the graffiti she'd noticed earlier. Several moments later the tunnel ended, and she found herself in a nondescript hallway painted white and devoid of graffiti.

"The lab is this way," Dr. Sylvester said, pointing ahead.

After unlocking another white door and climbing more steps, Nozomi found herself in an area that resembled Dr. Ash's lab in London. However, this man's lab appeared to have been repurposed from something else entirely. Nozomi thought the lab might have been part of the city's transit office.

In any case, there were many similarities between the two

doctors; both operated out of secret locations in the city, and both worked on enhancing humans. She made a mental note to discuss Dr. Sylvester Javitts with Dr. Ash.

"Up here," Dr. Sylvester said, pointing to a ladder.

Nozomi followed him, and she couldn't believe her eyes. She saw cyborgs in various stages of completion, many more were in tanks.

"I'm still trying to perfect the skin. I use the tanks to grow synthetic skin, and then I apply grafting techniques. The cyborgs in this room are my best work, and you are so much more advanced. You can pass for human. They cannot," the doctor said.

"So, what do you hope to solve by bringing me here?" Nozomi asked.

"Are you in contact with your creator?"

"What difference does that make?"

"It might make all the difference to me. I was hoping to collaborate with another creator. Perhaps we can learn from one another. Would you be willing to make an introduction?"

"Why would I want to do that?"

Dr. Sylvester flushed. He suddenly slammed his fist against a nearby table. "I don't understand why you won't just help. Don't you have any compassion left in you?"

Nozomi gave the doctor a wicked grin.

It's not wise to show weakness to a stranger.

She turned away and started walking.

"Wait!" Dr. Sylvester called. "I have some technology to trade—something your creator doesn't have."

"What's that?" Nozomi whirled around. "My creator has everything she needs—can't you see?" Nozomi spread her arms to emphasize the point.

"I have mastered the manufacturing of imprinting data cores," he said. "Few know as much as I do."

"You seem sure of yourself. You sound like you invented them."

The doctor smiled. "I may have had something to do with the process."

Dr. Ash needs data cores to continue her experiments and make us better.

The doctor started rummaging through drawers until he found another key. He pushed against a nearby bookcase, and it separated from the wall. Then the doctor reached into the wall and took out a small box, unlocked it, and gave it to Nozomi. A clear crystal about an inch long and half an inch wide was resting on velvet. She picked up the crystal, and it illuminated with a pale-blue glow.

"What is this?"

"A fully upgraded data core. It's the most advanced ever made. Help me perfect the skin, and I will teach your creator how to make more."

Nozomi hesitated. The doctor motioned toward the crystal.

"Take it," he said. "Think of it as a goodwill gesture. A token of the start of a fruitful relationship."

Nozomi took the data core. She couldn't be sure, but this one felt heavier and larger than any of the others she had removed from other cyborgs. She thanked the doctor for the gift and allowed him to escort her out of the maze that was the doctor's lab.

CHAPTER 6

Dr. Sylvester attempted to reach Riku by phone no less than ten times. He was about to give up when he finally got a text reply saying he was running late.

I give the kid fifty grand, and he ghosts me.

About two hours later, Riku showed up looking disheveled. His hair was sticking up in awkward places, and his clothes were wrinkled. He looked like he'd slept in the back of a car.

"Where have you been the past couple of days?" the doctor asked.

"I . . . had a family emergency, but I'm here for you, doctor."

The doctor gave Riku a hard look.

"I need your help with the new cyborg you brought in the other day," he told Riku. "Here is a list of items we need to complete the procedure. Meet me in the lab when you are ready."

About thirty minutes later, Riku arrived in the lab with the cybernetic implants Dr. Sylvester had asked for.

"Riku, please look for some empathy receptors the next time you are scavenging. I think our patient will need them in the future."

"Sure thing, Doc."

The doctor and Riku prepared for the procedure.

"This will involve some cutting. Are you able to assist?" Dr. Sylvester asked.

"I'm not as squeamish as I used to be," Riku replied. "I still get a little bothered when you dig those data cores out, but everything else I've gotten used to."

"You have steady hands. Have you considered a career in the medical profession?"

"I can't afford the tuition. My mother and aunt had to move in with me, so it's tough right now."

"Of course. Well, if you bring me more intact specimens like this, I will keep paying you for your efforts."

About an hour later, the surgery was complete. The doctor had replaced much of the cyborg's circuitry around the facial area. The data core and cybernetic brain were intact, so no additional work was necessary.

"Is it time to wake her up?" Riku asked.

"Almost. We need to give her an infusion of nutrients as soon as she comes online. She's been offline for several days. Her skin has decayed, and even with the treatments, the skin will continue deteriorating unless we bring her online now." Dr. Sylvester passed Riku a piece of paper. "Here is a list of food high in amino acids. I need for you to get these as quickly as you can."

"Whoa, you have caviar on the list!" Riku exclaimed. "That might take some time."

"Not if you know where to look." The doctor made a couple swiping gestures on his tablet. "I have sent you the name and location of a woman who has it, as well as the requisite Digibit to buy some."

"I will work on this now," Riku said as he left the lab.

Meanwhile, back at the Meadowlands

Treeka awoke to a single ray of sunlight shining on her face. Everything was foggy and disconnected. She thought she was in a certain hotel room in London, awaiting her sister's arrival. Despite Treeka's reservations, Meeka had wanted to go clubbing the night before. The evening had ended in disaster. The next memory she had was awakening as a cyborg.

"Meeka, she's out there . . . somewhere," Treeka said to the empty room.

Where am I? How did I get here?

Treeka got up and opened the window. The room was drenched in sunlight. People walked dogs and washed their cars. And children—there were children on the street. She stared in fascination for a moment. Treeka realized she was in a normal suburban neighborhood. That gave her hope.

I feel weak.

A system message appeared:

Nutrient levels critical, seek food and fluids immediately.

Where is my AI?

Treeka tried to access the system menus that controlled her internal AI interface. Another message appeared:

Too few system resources available for AI to function.

Treeka's vision blurred. The room spun. She fell to her knees and screamed in pain.

Moments later, Junior and another woman that Treeka didn't recognize entered the room.

"What's wrong?" Junior said.

"My body is failing."

Junior looked like he'd been punched in the gut.

"She doesn't look so good," Spirit said.

"Her cyborg body requires nutrients. I remember she ate caviar and fish at the party. That seemed to give her a boost."

"Well, it's a good thing I went to the grocery store this morning. Let's get her something to eat."

"Take me to food," Treeka said in a slurred voice.

Junior helped her to the kitchen table. Treeka collapsed in a chair while Spirit ripped through the cupboards.

"I know I have some of those fishy bastards . . . somewhere," Spirit said.

"What are you talking about?" Junior asked.

"Ahh, here they are. Sardines. You mentioned fish, and this is what I have."

Spirit put a generous portion of the fish in a bowl and put it in front of Treeka. The cyborg didn't respond. She stared at the sardines.

"What's the matter?" Junior asked.

Treeka picked up the sardine. It fell out of her hands. Junior picked it up and put it in her mouth. Treeka chewed in slow motion. It was like watching a turtle eat.

"Chop it up," Spirit said. "She's losing energy, so mashing the sardines into a paste might allow her to swallow easier and absorb the food faster."

Junior grabbed the bowl of sardines and found a large spoon. He began mashing up the sardines; it generated a good amount of juice. Then he scooped up the paste and fed it to her. She got as much of the fish substance on herself as she did in her mouth, as she was having a tough time chewing.

Treeka closed her eyes. Another system message appeared: *Nutrient levels at ten percent and rising.*

"Water? I need some water," Treeka said in a weak voice.

Junior fetched some tap water and gave it to her. Treeka gulped it down, much of it spilling over her naked body. For a moment, Junior seemed lost.

"Quit staring at her breast and pour her another glass of water," Spirit said.

Junior fetched the water, then watched Treeka finish it in another few gulps. Moments later, she asked for more sardines. The feeding process seemed to last an eternity, but Treeka was slowly feeling more like herself. She checked her nutrient levels; they were at fifty-eight percent and rising.

"That is enough for now," Treeka said.

No sooner than the words were out of her mouth than she started shivering. Treeka reached out and touched Junior's hand. It was beyond chilly; it felt frozen.

"She's cold, get her something to wear," Junior said.

Spirit ran to the bedroom and found a robe. The garment was several sizes too large, but he got Treeka into it. Treeka's eyes fluttered, but she kept shivering.

System Message:

Temperature control damaged at forty-five percent. Please raise body temperature.

"So cold," Treeka said.

Spirit helped Treeka get into more clothes; that seemed to stabilize Treeka enough to stop the onslaught of system messages she was getting.

"Need to find Meeka," Treeka blurted.

"Who's Meeka—?"

"Her sister," Junior said, interrupting Spirit. "Vince dumped her body somewhere between Little Italy and Chinatown."

"We can be there in an hour," Spirit said.

"That was days ago, and she might not be there, anyway."

"Why not?" Spirit demanded.

"We left her body in an area frequented by Doc Chop and his scavengers."

"Well, I think we should at least try to look."

"Spirit, call home base and see if we can borrow an engineer who can hack into security camera footage. We need to see who took Meeka's body," Junior said.

"I still think we should canvas the area," Spirit said.

"You do that, but I'm staying put. I've crossed some powerful people," Junior said.

Spirit removed her cap and combed a hand through her hair.

"I'll call for an engineer," she said.

Later that evening, somewhere in the underground

Riku entered Dr. Sylvester's underground lab. He noticed moisture buildup on the walls. Several drip marks had made inroads into the layers of caked dirt, giving the lab an added sinister look that made Riku uncomfortable.

"Did you get it?" Dr. Sylvester asked.

"I got it alright, that crazy bitch made me sit through tea. One companion was the mummified corpse of her sister," Riku said.

Dr. Sylvester snatched the items from Riku's hands and started looking through them.

"She has a corpse in her apartment?" Dr. Sylvester muttered. "Are you serious?"

"Either the caviar woman stole the corpse from a morgue, or it's a very good replica of one," Riku said, shuddering.

"Ahh. Daphne is a little esoteric, but she has a line on the best caviar in the city."

"I hope you don't need any more caviar, because she creeps

me out." Riku shuddered again at the memory. "So, what's next?"

"The caviar's consistency will make it easier to liquify," Dr. Sylvester replied. "When you were gone, I performed a full-body examination. Her primary intake of food is not from her mouth. She uses nutrition cartridges. However, I should be able to get the caviar into the right consistency for it to work like a nutrition cartridge."

"Is it time to wake her?" Riku asked.

"It's time to begin the post-operative procedure. We will be giving her an infusion of nutrients, but we have to be careful not to overload her system. Doing so may cause some erratic behavior."

"What do you need?"

"Fetch two bags of saline for the IV drip, and I will get the medicine. Meet back here in ten minutes," Dr. Sylvester said.

Riku watched the doctor leave; he had to make sure he was out of sight. Then he moved a chair to the other side of the circular lab. After using the chair as a makeshift ladder, he moved a lose title with a hole in it. A camera with a direct line of sight to Dr. Sylvester's operating table was tucked away. He replaced the battery and memory cards with fresh ones, then put it back in its place.

As he climbed off the chair, he froze. The cyborg was sitting upright and staring at him. She had the blank stare of someone who was in shock or sleepwalking.

"Are you alright?" Riku said hesitantly.

The cyborg didn't respond. Riku heard shuffling. The doctor stopped at the entrance to the lab.

"Fascinating," Dr. Sylvester said.

"What did you do? Did you work on her when I was gone?" Riku asked.

"No, but I think the response is involuntary." The doctor

put a hand in front of her face. When she didn't respond, he took a small flashlight out of his pocket and examined her eyes. "It's like she's in a coma." He put the flashlight back and turned back toward the door. "I will be right back—I still need to get the medicine." The doctor waved as he left.

Riku continued his preparations, but he kept a wary eye on the cyborg.

About twenty minutes later, the doctor added an injection of something in the IV connected to the cyborg's arm.

"The IV will help keep her fluid levels constant. She's organic, and she's subject to the same limitations as the rest of us carbon-based life-forms," Dr. Sylvester told Riku.

The doctor removed a side panel from the metal part of her torso, then inserted the cartridge filled with some inky black goo. He attached several electrodes on her head and other areas of her body.

"Wait, why the electrodes?" Riku asked. "Are we performing some kind of electroshock therapy?"

"We need to provide a small jolt to jump-start her system. She will start absorbing the nutrients much faster that way," Dr. Sylvester said. "Now, secure the patient."

Riku used the straps on the operating table to restrain the cyborg.

"Whatever happens," the doctor said, "make sure she stays strapped in."

Riku nodded as Dr. Sylvester powered up a machine next to the table. A low humming noise emanated from the machine. He turned a dial, then flipped some switches. The sound became louder, and Riku had a tough time concentrating on anything. The cyborg convulsed; Riku noticed that one of the straps loosened from the sudden movement. As he attempted to tighten the strap, it became looser, and then her cold hand was around his neck. He had trouble breathing as she squeezed.

"Doctor—" Riku gasped.

"Stop this at once!" the doctor yelled at the cyborg.

To Riku's surprise, she obeyed.

"She almost popped my cybernetic implants," Riku said.

The cyborg frowned, then froze. Her actions seemed programmatic, like she was performing a series of actions without thought. With the doctor's help, Riku secured her arm to the table and checked the other restraint.

Riku rubbed his neck; it was sore to the touch. If he looked in a mirror, he would no doubt notice some bruising. The rest of the procedure was carried out without further incident.

Nozomi entered her hideaway: a small room in a sleazy hotel in the Flatiron District of New York. Junkies and others looking to party often broke into her room. If they looked clean and had an open mind, they could persuade her to have a little recreation, but those opportunities were rare. Other than a few clothes and some toys, she kept nothing in her room. She went to the mirror and used her cybernetic interface to call Dr. Ash, who appeared to Nozomi in simulated three-dimensional space. The mirror allowed Dr. Ash to see Nozomi through her eyes.

"Nozomi, do you have any news for me?" Dr. Ash asked.

"The doctor we spoke of gave me a data core as a gesture of good faith," Nozomi said as she held the data core to the mirror.

"Excellent news, I will authenticate it once we are together," Dr. Ash said.

"The doctor is expecting me to give him the formula for the skin."

Dr. Ash put a virtual hand against her chin; it looked like she was in deep thought.

"I'm not comfortable giving him everything until I authenticate the data core, but I will give him most of it. Complete the trade understanding that more is to come later. I will record a standard greeting and data package for the doctor," Dr. Ash said.

"What do you want me to do after the trade?" Nozomi asked.

"Return to me in Newport. When can I expect you?"

"Considering it's a four-hour drive from the city and I have some loose ends to tie up, tomorrow at the earliest."

"I will expect your arrival—we have much to discuss," Dr. Ash said as she disconnected.

Moments later, Nozomi received the information Dr. Ash had promised. She opened a pouch on her belt and removed a thin cable with a USB connection on one side and a fiber-optic connection on the other. She tapped four times on the area behind her ear, just below the hairline, and a small panel was revealed. She plugged in the fiber-optic half of the cable into the interface, then plugged a flash drive into the USB port. Once the information was transferred, she prepared to meet with Doc Chop one last time.

CHAPTER 7

MEANWHILE, somewhere in the underground

The cyborg was lying atop a metal table, her arms and legs bound by leather straps. She appeared to be offline, sleeping, or whatever cyborgs classified as rest. Riku checked for a pulse. It was there, but it was faint.

"She is stable now. I gave her something to help her rest," the doctor said, looking at his watch. "Let's save the cleanup until tomorrow."

Riku nodded. "I'm exhausted."

"Before you leave, I'll give you tomorrow's shopping list. I will need you to pick up a few items for me on your way in tomorrow."

Riku followed Dr. Sylvester to his office. Despite being underground, the doctor took residence in an old transit maintenance office; it had only gone unnoticed because of an extra wall, built during the city's last remodeling project, that concealed its presence.

"You can retrieve the items at Seaport Village," the doctor instructed. "Someone will meet you at 7:15 tomorrow morning, so don't be late."

The doctor handed Riku a list. To anyone else it may have

seemed like the random scribblings of a madman, but Riku knew better. The doctor was the sanest person who Riku knew. However, not too many people he knew asked for goat kidneys, lamb tongues, or an ox heart. Riku shrugged as he pocketed the list.

"I will leave well before sunrise, as the Seaport is in the opposite direction, but consider it done," Riku said as he headed for the door.

Images of the female cyborg captivated him as he took a familiar route to the surface. Drops of water dripped on his head as he ascended the many tunnels and ladders, but he barely noticed. Despite the cyborg's attack, Riku found himself attracted to her charms. He was almost at the surface of the subterranean labyrinth that was Doc Chop's world when he remembered something important.

Dammit, I forgot to get the memory card. Mr. Payne is going to pay out the ass for this footage.

To his knowledge, no one had caught the awakening of a cyborg on tape. Riku changed the memory card in his hidden camera every day, and his nights were often spent scrubbing through hours of footage. He didn't want to risk leaving such good footage to chance. His stomach churned at the thought of entering the lab alone, whether the cyborg was tied up or not. After a moment of indecision, he headed back to the lab.

Riku entered the darkened lab. Dr. Sylvester's patient appeared to be resting on the operating table. He moved the chair over to his secret hiding spot, just like he'd done so many times before. After removing the tile from the wall, he took a moment to check the battery level after he swapped out the memory card. Riku always kept a spare battery on hand, and he didn't want to risk running out of juice at a critical moment. He determined it had enough of a charge to last a few more days. After replacing the memory chip he was about to leave when he heard rustling.

"Who are you going to sell the footage to?" a female voice said.

Roku looked around. No one was there.

I must be hearing things.

"I can help you," the voice persisted.

The volume of the voice filled the room. Riku jumped, then dropped the tile. It shattered into a million pieces. He shone a light toward the direction of the voice. The cyborg remained on the table, restraints intact. He walked over and tested the restraints again, just to be sure. The cyborg was alert and watching his every move.

I must be exhausted—there is no way she is trying to communicate with me.

"No?" the voice asked. "But I am trying to communicate."

"There is no way you're talking after the sedative," Riku said.

"I'm not talking with my mouth, but with my mind. For a smart guy you can be quite dense, but you're kind of cute."

"How it is possible? That you are speaking with your mind, I mean."

"It's a talent my sister helped me with. We share a connection, since we are twins. As far as I know, I don't share anything with you. But, if there is anyone who can figure out why we have this connection, it's you."

"The doctor gave you a drug to help you sleep—you should be out cold."

"I suspect the good doctor doesn't know as much as he lets on. I'm still conscious, but I cannot move my body."

"That's incredible!" Riku said as he retested the cyborg's restraints.

"You don't need to worry, I wish you no harm. But I need you to do something for me."

"I don't know . . . Dr. Sylvester will fire me if I go behind his back. I need this job, and you are important to him."

"I'm sure I am, but the doctor's lust will have to wait."

"Lust?"

"You don't know?"

"I know I don't know what you're talking about."

"While you were away—fetching parts, I think—the doctor was having his way with me."

"Oh, I'm sorry you had to endure that."

"Thanks, Riku. You are a perfect gentleman. I need to contact my sister, but I have no way of doing so. Do you think you can get her a message?"

"Who is your sister?"

"Her name is Treeka. Tell her that her sister is in danger, and she will come looking for me."

"I don't even know how to contact her."

"Before our team leader betrayed us, we received an upgrade—"

"Betrayed?" Riku interrupted.

"Yes. Nozomi had her pet shoot me point-blank in the face. I don't even know how I got here."

"I found you . . . in a dumpster near Chinatown," Riku said hesitantly. "What do you know about the upgrade?"

"I remember only one detail about that connection. A string of numbers separated by dots."

Is she referring to an IP address? Riku wondered.

"Can you tell me the numbers?" he asked.

"2.223.47.91 are the numbers. Do you know what they mean?"

"That is an IP address."

"I do not know what that is," the cyborg said.

"It's like a street address for the internet. I should be able to pinpoint the location. It's the server someone connected you to. Maybe it was the address to an artificial intelligence."

"If you can contact Treeka in that way, we can be together again. I'm afraid of what this doctor is going to do to me. Can you help?"

Why does this thing want my help? Maybe I can use her to my advantage. I will pretend—for now.

Riku looked at the cyborg for a long moment. Tears started flowing from her eyes.

"Okay," he said, "I will help you. What's your name? If I can reach your sister, she probably will want me to confirm your name."

"My name is Meeka."

"It's good to meet you, Meeka."

"Please contact her."

Riku took one of the cyborg's hands and gave a light squeeze. He couldn't explain it, but her touch aroused him.

She's electrifying. No wonder why the doctor wants her.

"I will, I promise," Riku said as he left.

Somewhere between Long Island and Connecticut

Sally Wilde fetched her laptop from the battered desk and headed outside. It was a clear brisk afternoon, and she was tired of being in the hangar. Her father, Damien Wilde, was in charge of the Dark Angels, a group of freedom fighters and outlaws who worked on the fringe. She approached a weathered metal table that served as her preparation area. She was responsible for testing and maintaining the drones the Dark Angels used for their reconnaissance work.

Sally bit her lip as she uploaded the latest version of the firmware to the drone she was working on. A light breeze blew her long blond hair across her face. She pulled her hair back and tied it up so she could work. The fall day brought the promise of more chilly weather.

I've been working on this for weeks—this better not screw up now.

The airplane hangar that had been her father's base of operations made for a poor working and living environment. Being the daughter of a Dark Angel required a lot of commitment and sacrifice. She often wondered what it would be like to grow up in a normal home.

I need to get this tested before the strike team moves in. It's the ultimate piece of the puzzle.

Sally carried the heavy drone away for some high-altitude testing. She placed it on the ground and made sure it was turned on. After checking the firmware and battery levels, she prepared for liftoff. She noticed a slight wobble on the right side of the craft, but she would have enough time to fix it before it was needed for her father's next mission. The drone ascended to more than a thousand feet before she enabled the onboard cameras. The drone featured a three-hundred-and-sixty-degree view of its surroundings; however, it was blind above and below.

I need to add more cameras.

She tested each zoom lens on the camera. Each offered a twenty-times zoom factor and had its own memory card. This meant the drone could record six streams of video at the same time. She had some scarecrows that served as targets at the other end of the island, some two thousand feet away. When

Sally was confidant she had tested each camera, she piloted the drone back to safety.

"You're going to make a superb pilot someday," a gruff voice said.

A smile formed on Sally's face.

"Hello, Father. Don't you have better things to do than watch your daughter play with her toys?"

She turned to see a man in his late forties with an eye patch. He had an enormous tattoo of a dragon with a serpent in its claws on his left bicep.

"That is not a toy," Damien Wilde said, pointing to the drone. "It's a precision instrument piloted by one of the most capable people I know."

Sally blushed. Her father didn't give compliments, not to her. She knew it had been difficult for him to raise her alone, and she always made certain to pull her own weight. The Dark Angels was a family operation, and she often had to set the example for the recruits.

Sometimes I wish my father weren't the head of the Dark Angels. Maybe I would have had a normal childhood.

"Will that thing be ready for our operation on the Windowless Building? I know Titus is eager to test a few theories."

"I need to make adjustments for a slight wobble and add two more cameras, but it will be ready soon enough."

"Good, because a friend of the Angels has cashed in one of his favors. Are you up for a trip to Meadowlands?"

"What's going on there?"

"All I know is it involves hacking, and you are the best hack —I mean *engineer* we have."

"Give me an hour to make the adjustments to this drone, then I'll be ready."

Marty Payne detested technology, which was ironic since he made millions off his desire to exploit it. He gazed out of the eightieth-floor penthouse he'd acquired under an assumed name. He owned many sanctuaries in the city. The apartment off Fifth Avenue was his official address, but he grew tired of being hounded by the press and the people it attracted, so he avoided it for now.

I am the invisible man when I want to be. Marty chuckled.

He rummaged in his pocket and removed a memory chip. It took some effort, but he could free it from its protective casing.

I'm glad Riku came through again. He's expensive, but he provides eighty percent of the content for the Amateur Sleuths *channel.*

Marty examined the camera memory chip. It was hard to fathom the piece of plastic and silicon was worth millions. He had so much money that he couldn't spend it all in three lifetimes. And all his wealth had not provided happiness or solace.

I think it's time to get my hands on my own cyborg. Perhaps I can reach out to this doctor and make a deal? It's going to be tricky, but I think I can make it happen. I just need something he wants . . . desires.

Marty transferred the new batch of videos his contact had provided. Two men were in the frame: his primary contact, Riku, who had sold him the videos; and the doctor, who experimented on many of the poor souls who wished to become cyborgs. Although the audio was often poor, he could clean it up enough to hear what was being said. One woman begged to be killed after one of the doctor's failed cybernetic experiments. He would respond by performing more experiments—or, if the targets were the right gender and age, he would take his pleasure on their screaming bodies before dispatching them. The more pain his victims were in, the more he seemed to enjoy himself. Marty paused the video.

I'd better watch myself around this guy, otherwise I might end up like one of these wretches.

Marty resumed the video. The assistant left to fetch some item while the doctor undressed the cyborg that was lying helpless on the table. He loosened the restraints of the cyborg's legs. The minutes of footage that followed he could not use on his video streaming service—not unless he wanted to be known for hardcore cyborg snuff.

This doctor is one sick fuck.

Marty skipped ahead to find something useful when he spotted something: an image on the doctor's tablet. The doctor appeared to be having a conversation with himself in the lab while pointing to the tablet; Marty could only make out fragments of what he was saying. The image looked like a glowing crystal, and it gave him an idea.

What did the doctor call it? He rewound the video and listened again. *A core?*

Marty tried cleaning up the audio, but there was too much interference. If he could get his hands on some footage of the doctor extracting or inserting one of these cores into a cyborg, that would add another unique element to the show; it would elevate his channel even higher. Not to mention it would also increase his subscriber count.

Now, where is Riku's number?

CHAPTER 8

ANGEL'S ISLAND, somewhere off the coast of Connecticut

"Hey, Sally, where you headed?" the boy asked.

"Father is sending me to the Meadowlands," she replied. "Apparently, there's something important to hack."

"Just take care of yourself."

The boy was about the same age as Sally. She knew he cared for her, but she didn't share his feelings. All she wanted to do was complete the job her father had assigned her and get back to the hangar to prepare for her first field mission.

"If Damien is sending you, it must be important," the boy said. "I hope you're ready for the assault on the infamous windowless building. It will be legendary."

"Don't worry, Chip, I wouldn't miss it for the world," Sally said as Chip left the hangar.

Damien Wilde, Sally's father, was waiting for her just outside the hangar door.

"Here to see me off, Father?"

"I know you don't turn eighteen until the end of the month," he said, "but I'm proud of the woman you have become."

"That's a relief, Father."

"What I'm trying to say is, be careful."

Damien hugged Sally—rare and out of character for her father. She couldn't remember the last time he'd shown his true feelings.

"Is there anything I should know before I head to the Meadowlands?" Sally asked.

"Junior, the person who called us, saved my life when I was a young man. Desert Storm was our first deployment. We were pinned down in Khafji. It was my first time seeing any kind of action. If he had not come to our rescue, I may have died."

Sally nodded. She couldn't remember the last time her father had even talked about his time in the military.

"I wanted you to know what kind of man Junior is. He is —was a member of the Lombarto crime family. He must be in trouble if he called in this chit. I trust him, but just keep your guard up, just in case there are members of the Lombarto family in the area. Spirit is already there, and Cherub will escort you to the safe house."

Sally responded by giving her father a hug. He reluctantly returned the affection.

It's alright to show emotion, Father. It's been more than ten years since Mother passed.

Sally boarded the helicopter and watched her father fade away as she ascended.

It took more than an hour to get to the private landing strip near the Meadowlands. Cherub secured the helicopter, then checked the condition of their ground transportation. She removed the tarp from the classic muscle car. Sally climbed into the passenger seat and watched the sun set as Cherub drove to the safe house.

"Do you know Junior?" Sally asked.

"Only by reputation," Cherub replied.

"My father spoke highly of him. I think he saved his life in the war."

"Desert Storm was a long time ago, and people change. I briefly saw Junior the other night . . ." Cherub trailed off.

"What is it?"

"It wasn't him, it was his companion. She was different—and not because she was naked, either."

"Different, how?"

"I don't think she is completely human."

"What are you saying? She's a cyborg or something?"

Cherub shot Sally a look. They rode the rest of the way in silence. The safe house was in an ordinary residential neighborhood. It looked normal in every way, but Sally wiped away the perspiration that made her palms sweat.

Calm down. The job is probably nothing more than hacking into some crime boss's computer. You can do that in your sleep.

Cherub escorted her inside the house. An enormous man, more than six feet tall, was sitting on the couch next to a woman who looked ill.

"This is Sally Wilde, Damien's daughter," Spirit said to the man on the couch.

The enormous man got up from the couch, then shook Sally's hand.

"It's good to meet you, I'm Junior. I can't remember the last time I saw you. You were just a toddler. You look so much like your mother."

"You knew my mother?" Sally asked.

"Yes, she was my baby sister. You can call me Uncle Junior."

Sally was speechless. Silence hung in the air.

Why didn't Father mention this? Or is this guy full of shit? I'd better just do the work and leave.

"What do I need to hack?" Sally asked, eager to change the subject.

"We need to find Meeka, my sister," Treeka said.

What's the matter with her? Is she sick? Sally thought. *I have a bad feeling about this.*

Sally felt all the moisture from her mouth evaporate.

Junior introduced the cyborg to Sally and briefly explained their predicament. Treeka's robe shifted for a moment, and Sally got a glimpse of the cyborg's metal torso.

"If I understand correctly, we have two tasks here," Sally said. "To find a doctor who can work on cyborgs, and find her sister as well?" Sally looked at Treeka; she appeared sad, like she'd lost her only friend.

"Which task is the priority?" Sally asked.

"We need to figure out how to refill these." Junior showed Sally a cylinder. It looked like a metal tube with glass in the middle.

"What's that?"

"It's the source of Treeka's nutrition. It normally contains some condensed version of food that is ingested from a compartment on the metal side of her torso," Junior explained.

"We tried feeding her regular food like fish, but it's a slow process," Spirit said.

"So we need the doctor to refill the metal tube?"

"I didn't mention that in the request, but I want to talk to the doctor first."

"I need an area to get set up," Sally said.

Spirit gave Sally the information for the house Wi-Fi and, about an hour later, Sally had a complete dossier on two possible cyborg doctor candidates.

"I was able to find two doctors who have degrees in genetic engineering. One of them has a degree in robotics as well," she said.

"Tell us about the robot doc," Junior said.

"Dr. Sylvester Javitts is his real name, but he is known as Doc Chop around the city's underworld."

"Do you know how to contact him?"

"He's off the grid, but according to the chatter I've seen on the dark web, he has a proxy that might be able to arrange a meeting."

"Okay. I don't know about any of you, but the nickname of Doc Chop sounds ominous. What about the other doctor?" Spirit asked.

"His name is Doctor Nicolai Brody, but I don't know if you want to use him."

"Why not?"

"In addition to eight counts of genetic modification on aborted fetuses, he is also wanted for sexual assault."

Junior gave Treeka a look.

"Let's try to reach out to this Doc Chop," Junior said.

Sally began typing furiously into her computer. "I've reached out to the proxy, but it might be a while before he responds."

"Find Meeka," Treeka said.

"Do you have a photo, or even a last name?" Sally asked the cyborg. "I need something else to go on."

"Her actual name is Misato Kiyomizu," Treeka replied.

It took Sally a bit longer to find any information on Misato. She tried accessing various databases, including the DMV, and only found records of her demise.

"Something's wrong. According to DMV records in all fifty states, I'm not finding any current records. But I did find a death certificate."

Treeka explained they had been involved in a car accident and then legally declared dead. She mentioned how Dr. Elizabeth Ash had restored their minds into cyborg constructs that looked like their former selves, but were different.

"Why don't we get in touch with this Dr. Ash?" Sally asked. "If she created you, then she must know how to help you."

"She betrayed us. She is our enemy now."

It's getting late, and I don't think I can help her, Sally thought.

Sally was about to shut her laptop down when an encrypted message appeared in her dark web mailbox. The message read:

Dear WildChild,

Thank you for reaching out. You are correct in assuming I'm the doctor's only proxy. I will facilitate a meeting, but it will cost ten Digibit. Please reply with the Digibit, and I will send you the location for the meet.

The message was signed with the letter "R."

"It looks like we have our doctor's appointment. Who wants to send me ten Digibit coins?" Sally asked.

"How much is a coin?" Junior asked.

"$7,214.44 at current prices."

"That's more than seventy-two thousand dollars," Junior said, exasperated.

"Well, you can't expect a high school girl to have that kind of money," Sally said.

Junior pulled out his smartphone and transferred the amount into Sally's account.

"I will let you handle the conversion, just get us a meeting," Junior said.

Sally did as the message had asked and, an hour later, received a confirmation for the meeting.

"You are to take your cyborg to Battery Park at three a.m.

Near the carousel. Use the code word *torment*," Sally told Junior and Spirit.

"Tonight?" Junior asked. "That's less than two hours!"

"Here are the details. I need to get back to the hangar," Sally said, transferring the information to Junior's phone.

"I think we got it from here. Take care of yourself, kid, and say hi to your old man," Junior said.

"I will walk you out," Spirit said, following Sally and Cherub.

Outside, Cherub took out a cigarette and passed one to Sally. She looked back at the house, then took a step toward the car.

"That thing . . . creeps me out," Sally said as she lit up.

"The cyborg?" Cherub replied. "I don't like to judge, but there's more to it than that. Did you see how Junior looks at her? It's like they are in love." He paused to take a drag. "I've spent time with both of them—Junior broke her out of a hostile situation. They were dodging bullets as they escaped with their lives."

Sally took another drag from her cigarette.

"Be careful, Spirit, you don't want to end up in a dumpster somewhere."

Cherub pulled Spirit close. "That will not happen so long as I'm around."

"Don't worry, kid, I've been through much worse. From what I hear, Damien's sending you on your first mission soon. How do you feel about that?" Spirit asked.

That's a good question. I should be fucking terrified, but I don't feel anything.

"I feel fine. The other engineers will be there too—each of us has an important job. Hell, I trained most of them," Sally said.

Spirit gave Sally a sympathetic look. "Don't worry, kid, you'll do okay."

Cherub opened the car door for Sally. As she got in, she noticed the affection the couple shared. As with everyone in the Dark Angels, they shared a bond that had been forged from extreme circumstances.

When Riku was certain the doctor had retired for the evening, he sneaked into the lab to find a restrained Meeka lying naked on the table.

"Did you find Treeka?" Meeka asked.

"Yes, I think so. The IP address—I mean, that string of numbers separated by dots—was traceable to several locations across the city," Riku said.

"What does that mean? Do you know where Treeka is or not?"

"I know where she is. She's in a house in New Jersey, near the Meadowlands. I could trace it that far. Also, moments ago I replied to a dark web forum. Apparently someone needs help with something very similar to your nutrition cartridge. I will meet with them later tonight."

"Good work, Riku," Meeka said.

"Once I deliver Treeka, you need to do something for me," Riku said.

"Anything, just name it."

"I'm going to be leaving the city, and I need you to protect me. The doctor has people he will send after me if I just bolt. We will leave by boat tomorrow—there's room for you and Treeka."

"I accept," Meeka said. "Now come here and let me reward you. But you will need to remove these restraints first."

Riku complied. Meeka rubbed her arms and legs and then leaped off the table.

"Where are you going?" Riku asked.

"Nowhere, I'm just getting the blood flowing again. Now, take your clothes off and lay down on the table. I will take care of the rest."

Riku did as he was told.

What the hell am I doing?

Riku was conflicted; he wanted her more than any woman he'd ever known. The only sexual encounter he'd experienced had been brief, and his mother had interrupted it. Riku longed to be in his own place, but he would need to stay in the crowded apartment with his parents and grandparents for a little while longer. Soon he would be free.

"Let me help you," Meeka said.

She helped him remove his pants and shirt and threw them across the room. He felt both aroused and guilty standing next to a naked woman, wearing nothing more than his underwear. She leaned her body against his and kissed him. Her soft breast and cold metal torso pressed against his bare chest. She removed his underwear, and they embraced. The next sensation Riku felt was nothing like he had ever experienced.

Two hours later

The Battery, one of New York's oldest parks, was known to house all manner of nasty characters, especially after dark. Spirit dropped Junior and Treeka off near the park entrance closest to the carousel, and Junior scanned the area, looking for threats.

"We need to find Meeka," Treeka said.

"After we get you fixed up we will, but for now we need to find this doctor," Junior said.

The cyborg clung to Junior like her life depended on it as they followed the signs to the carousel. Moments later, the carousel—enclosed within a building resembling an enormous tin hat—came into view. Although the building was dark, Junior could see the misshapen figures of fish and dolphins through the massive glass windows. If the carousel's strange and eerie look didn't creep Junior out enough, the tall man dressed in a white suit who appeared out of the nearby shadows certainly did.

Is that man . . . grinning? Junior squinted.

The man in the white suit appeared to be at least seven feet tall and had a pale complexion; his look reminded Junior of an albino. As soon as Junior finished the thought, the man gazed up at the sky and raised his arms. Then he started to dance, arms outstretched. He looked like he was dancing with a ghost. The scene became creepier as a low fog wrapped around the nearby carousel.

Junior stopped about thirty feet from the carousel. Two sleeping homeless men occupied the nearby park benches; they appeared to be having difficulty sleeping, due to a divider in the middle of the bench. The man in the white suit started to spin while looking up at the night sky.

"What is that man doing?" Treeka asked.

"There's a lot of crazy people who come out after dark. The city has tried to keep them out, but the park is too big," Junior explained.

Moments later, a young man approached them. He looked like he was in his early twenties. He was dressed in a black hoodie and blue jeans.

"You looking for the doctor?" the newcomer asked.

Junior nodded.

"What is the magic word?"

"Torment," Junior said.

"Why do you need to see the doctor?"

When Junior didn't answer, the man turned to leave. "Fine, if you won't cooperate, the doctor has other patients to see," he said.

"Wait," Junior said. "My friend here has special needs. How will I know the doctor can even help her?"

The young man turned back and looked Treeka over for a long moment before answering.

"If her needs were common, then you would not have paid so much for an audience. The price for ten Digibit is quite high at current rates, and you didn't even try to negotiate, so let's cut the bullshit and tell me why you're here."

Junior gave the man an appraising look.

"She has certain needs that require the use of this." Junior removed Treeka's nutrition cartridge from his inside coat pocket. "We need a way to fill it that provides the nutrients she needs without resorting to shoving food down her throat."

"Well, I think I can help you, after all—or rather, help myself," the young man said, smiling.

The young man removed something from the front pocket of his hoodie, held it for a moment, and then pressed it like he was changing the channel on a remote control. The man seemed to disappear.

Junior heard some rustling from a nearby bush, but the fog obscured his view. He briefly considered looking for the young man when he noticed another problem; the man in the white suit was running toward Junior at a high rate of speed, faster than he thought humanly possible. Junior pulled his gun from his holster and prepared for the inevitable.

The man in the suit giggled like a deranged maniac as he held his hands out, palms up toward Junior. Small golf-ball-

sized objects appeared in the giggling man's hands like a magi-
cian performing some kind of crazy magic trick. Moments later,
the balls disappeared. The man's maniacal laughter increased
as he waved his palms in the air. Then he extended his arm
toward Junior and unleashed a torrent of golf balls, which
seemed to be shooting out of his sleeve. Junior dodged the
round projectiles. The maniac continued laughing as more of
the objects flew toward Junior's head. Treeka removed her
dagger and thrust it out in the maniac's direction. The man
continued laughing as he dodged her advances. One of the
homeless men awoke, sat up, and appeared to be watching the
fight.

The attacker's giggles turned into growls as Junior
continued to evade the man's blitzkrieg. Then the man in the
white suit focused his attack on the bum, who got pummeled by
one of the golf-ball-shaped objects; he screamed as acid began
melting through his clothes. The other bum jumped to his feet
and tried to run, so the attacking maniac slung a few more acid
balls at him. Somehow the man evaded the acid balls,
screaming in horror as he ran away. The other bum moaned as
he crawled away, clothes melted onto his skin.

"Stop this!" Treeka cried.

The maniac leaped onto the fallen bum's back, grabbed
him by the hair, and shoved an acid ball into his mouth. The
bum tried to scream, but the maniac held the bum's mouth
closed. Some kind of foamy substance poured from the bum's
nose and mouth. The maniac's fingers were covered with the
acid, but it didn't seem to hurt him.

How in the hell is this maniac avoiding the acid? Junior
wondered.

Junior tried to get a shot off, but the maniac seemed to
anticipate his movement and shot one of the acidic golf balls at
Junior's weapon. The acid ball hit the barrel with deadly preci-

sion, and the metal started to bubble and smoke. Junior threw the melting gun at the man, who caught it easily. Junior watched in horror as the metal melted in the man's hand, then he dodged more of the acid balls.

This man is not human—not completely, anyway.

Junior removed his coat, and knives of all sizes were visible. Many small blades were attached to his belt; he also had two large knives strapped to his back. He began removing the smaller knives and throwing them at the maniac acid-slinger. A couple of knives that should have penetrated the man's chest were deflected somehow, but at least one hit its intended target; a knife hit the maniac in the bicep, and greenish goo poured from the wound and onto his pristine white suit. Junior threw two more knives. One of them embedded in the man's chest, and another lodged in his throat. The man stumbled, then fell, clutching his neck. Junior approached him and decided to punt his head like a football, sending the man's head flying back. Junior heard a nasty crunching sound. The body convulsed a few times, then stopped.

"Let's go," Junior said to Treeka.

"I'm losing energy," she replied.

Junior picked up Treeka, then ran toward the street. He didn't know who these psychos had been, but he didn't want more to show up. Junior and Treeka made their way to the park entrance. The young man was there, waiting by an enormous SUV that was partially parked on the sidewalk. The tinted windows made it impossible to tell if anyone was inside the vehicle.

"Congratulations, you have earned an audience with the doctor," the young man said.

Junior put Treeka down and unsheathed a large machete.

"What? Is this some kind of sick joke?" Junior said.

"I'm afraid my employer is deadly serious. He is invested in the well-being of all cyborgs."

"Give me one good reason I shouldn't gut you like the swine you are," Junior said.

As if on cue, all the SUV's doors opened and several people who could only be described as freaks of nature filed out. One man, a tall and skinny man with green hair, was the first person out. He was wearing a leather jacket and some kind of stretchy pants. Several cybernetic implants were visible on his face, neck, and hands. The rest of him was covered with some kind of elastic material, but Junior suspected he bore many more hidden implants. Next to him was a large black man who resembled a linebacker. His left eye was covered with some kind of cybernetic monocle. His expensive-looking pinstriped suit was quite the contrast to the skinny man.

"I think we got off on the wrong foot," the young man said. "Dr. Sylvester has extended an invitation to his laboratory. It's rare he invites anyone into his inner sanctum, but you have defeated some of the strongest of us."

Junior put his blade away.

"So, we come with you?" he asked. "Just like that? No blindfolds or restraints?"

"Of course not. We want our guests to be comfortable. You can even keep your weapons at the ready if you desire."

Another smaller, middle-aged man handed Junior his coat that he'd discarded earlier. "I thought you would like this returned to you," he said. "It looks expensive."

Junior snatched his coat from the man's hand and put it around Treeka. He helped her into the vehicle, and the freak show followed his lead. Moments later, Treeka rested her head against Junior as the SUV traveled north along the West Side Highway.

Just after dawn, the SUV pulled up to a nondescript building off Broadway on the Upper West Side. Everyone got out, and Junior and Treeka followed the group toward the building. Soon the freaks and their guests descended a set of stairs near a corner market that had long gone out of business; faded posters of meat, eggs, and other food items were attached to the windows. Junior's nostrils were assaulted with the smell of urine and decay.

One of the young man's associates opened the door at the bottom of the staircase and stepped through. Junior and Treeka were then urged through the door. As soon as everyone was inside, the freak closed the door behind them. The room was partially lit, but Junior could make out who everyone was.

"Well, you must be the muscle that Riku was talking about," a man said.

Junior looked around for the source of the voice. After a moment, a tall man emerged from behind a group of freaks. He had salt-and-pepper hair, round glasses, and a graying goatee. He wore doctor's scrubs and a white lab coat.

"Are you the doctor?" Junior asked.

"Sorry for my lack of manners," the man said. "My name is Dr. Sylvester Javitts. And who might you be?"

"I'm Junior, and this is Treeka."

Junior noticed the young man flinched upon hearing her name.

"Do you think you can help us with this?" Junior asked as he produced the empty nutrition cartridge.

"Oh, it's been a while since I've seen one of these, but yes, I think I can help you," the doctor replied.

Junior noticed the young man who the doctor called "Riku"

had been looking at Treeka with some interest since learning her name.

There's something not quite right here, but I will play along . . . for now.

"Do you know how to get it open?" he asked the doctor. "I tried to open it but did not have any luck. Treeka tried eating food high in amino acids that would get absorbed by the body, but it didn't seem to give her the boost in energy."

"Since you are not an expert in cyborg physiology, then you do not know what food Treeka needs. I can help with that," the doctor replied.

"That would be appreciated."

The doctor took out a small flashlight, then shone it into Treeka's eyes. She squirmed away.

"Stop, it hurts," Treeka said.

"She's malnourished," Dr. Sylvester stated. "We need to get her the proper nutrients, and soon. Can you leave her here with me?"

"No," Treeka said as she took Junior's arm.

"I was hoping you could refill that cartridge for us and maybe provide some instruction on refilling it," Junior said.

"No, I'm afraid that is not possible, it's not like this is a simple procedure. I need her to perfect the mixture."

"Then I'm staying with her."

"I don't think we have enough room for the two of you, but maybe we can accommodate."

"Where will we be working?" Junior asked.

"Close by." The doctor considered for a moment. "Riku, please make arrangements at the Belmont for our guests."

"The Belmont? I'm not familiar with that hotel," Junior said, puzzled.

"It's close by, and I think you will like it there," Riku said.

"Good, because I think Treeka should rest—"

Junior was interrupted by something painful biting into his neck. It felt like a mosquito, but it wasn't. He turned to see the young man with a syringe in his hands.

This is a double cross—I will kill them.

Junior dropped to his knees as the effects of whatever Riku had injected him with took over. He tried fighting it, but a wave of blackness washed over him.

Treeka watched in horror as Junior dropped to the ground, then stopped moving.

"No!" Treeka said as she ran to Junior.

She was in a weakened state, but she managed to fend off the creeps who tried to pull her away from Junior. She checked his pulse; it was weak, but it was there.

"No need to worry, my dear, the big oaf is still alive. Even he has a part to play in the grand scheme of things," the doctor said.

"What should we do with her?" Riku asked.

"Take her to the lab."

Without warning, Riku injected Treeka with a sedative. In reaction, she removed the small knife from her pocket and thrust it toward Riku. She missed but stabbed the green-haired freak in the arm.

"Argh, you fucking bitch," the freak said as he backhanded her.

"Stop this, none of you are to harm her," the doctor demanded.

Treeka's vision blurred as she surrendered to the darkness.

CHAPTER 9

Hɪʀoᴛo ᴛooᴋ a hit from the hookah pipe as he considered his options. There weren't many people inside the lounge, so nobody was nearby. He closed his eyes as he inhaled the tobacco. He let the smoke penetrate his lungs for a moment before exhaling. Then the chirping sound of his phone ruined his moment of reflection; it was from Tsuyoshi Kiyomizu. Hiroto had lost his quarry days ago, and the worst part was telling his mentor—his master—the truth.

"Sensei," Hiroto said as he answered the phone.

"I'm eager to hear of your status," Tsuyoshi said.

"I tracked the mole to his lair, my sensei."

"Did your search of the mole's lair bear fruit?"

"It's heavily guarded. I'm still working out the best way to approach it," Hiroto said.

"Do you have any news on my girls?"

"No, the trail has gone cold."

Hiroto thought he could hear his master let out an impatient sigh.

"Then we will hunt your quarry together."

"You are coming to New York?" Hiroto asked.

"Yes," his mentor replied, "I have urgent business at one of my offices. Someone is attempting a hostile takeover at one of my subsidiaries. I hope you have a lead on Tomiju and Misato by then."

"I will await your arrival."

Later that evening
Hiroto received an in-visor notification. It was encrypted.
I hope this is from Sumoto.
The security settings on his AR interface required additional authentication to unlock the message. After performing the steps, he accessed the message, which read:

Here is the information I could find on the kid.
  Name: Riku (probably an alias, no surname available)
  Occupation: Systems Operator II
  Employer: Dr. Sylvester Javitts
  Side Employment: Submits videos for Amateur Sleuths Web Streaming
  Last known location: 91st and Broadway at 17:51 p.m.

Hiroto was excited. *That was less than three hours ago.*
He checked the message for additional information. After examining it multiple times, the message was clean, but an enormous blob of metadata was attached. He selected the scan file types option in his menu interface. Moments later, the blob was identified as a video file. He played the video; the suspect known as Riku was exiting a vehicle on 91st street near Broadway. A gigantic man was accompanying Hiroto's target, Tomiju Kiyomizu. He tapped on the image of Tomiju, and a mini

dossier displayed on his AR interface provided the following information:

Name: Tomiju Kiyomizu (a.k.a. Treeka)
  Height: 5 foot zero inches
  Eye Color: Gray
  Hair: Black
  Sibling: Misato Kiyomizu (a.k.a Meeka)

Hiroto brought his AI online. The slender image of a samurai warrior in his mid-twenties appeared in three-dimensional space; with the enhanced AR image, it was like the AI was actually standing in front of him.

"How can I help you, master?" the AI said.

"Kaen," Hiroto said, "locate the nearest motorcycle with a top speed of one hundred miles per hour."

"I've located a rare, limited edition Yamablaze cycle that was custom built by Japan's top automotive engineer. Would you like me to summon it?"

"You can do that?"

"Of course, master. The cycle has a one-of-a-kind navigation feature that can drive solo for a short distance."

"Yes, please summon the cycle. We will borrow it then return it to its rightful owner."

"The cycle will be outside your current Mott Street location in two point one seven minutes."

Hiroto stepped outside into the rain. Moments later, a low-profile motorcycle rounded a corner and stopped in front of him. It resembled a black angry hornet with sharp pointy angles. A black helmet was attached to the seat.

"Releasing safety features," the AI said.

An audible snapping noise emitted from the helmet as the buckle unlocked. He liberated it from the seat and put it on.

"I have switched manual control to you," Kaen said. "I estimate traffic to be moderate this time of the evening. If you take the West Side Highway at safe speeds, you should arrive at your intended destination in thirty-three minutes."

Let's shorten that to less than twenty.

Growing up in Tokyo, Hiroto was no stranger to high-powered motorcycles. He switched gears and applied just enough torque to allow him to glide down Mott Street toward Canal. Less than two minutes later, he was ripping down the West Side Highway in excess of eighty miles per hour.

"You should slow down, master. I sense police activity in your immediate area," Kaen said.

Twelve minutes later, Hiroto was exiting the 79th Street exit and heading east. After a harrowing left turn onto Broadway, he flew the remaining twelve blocks in less than a minute. He stopped in front of an abandoned market. Looking around, he recognized the staircase leading into oblivion from the camera footage. A pizza delivery car almost hit him as he crossed the street. The driver honked, then gave him the finger. Hiroto didn't have time for niceties; he needed to find Tomiju quick, because her father would fly in at any moment, and Hiroto would choose death before meeting Tsuyoshi empty-handed. He slapped the helmet on the back of the seat, and it locked into position.

"Kaen, deposit the cycle in a safe location, out of sight if possible," Hiroto ordered.

"Yes, master, I have the perfect location in mind," the AI replied as the bike ripped away, leaving more skid marks on the pavement. The cycle headed down Broadway for a couple of blocks, then turned west onto 89th Street toward the Hudson River.

Hiroto noticed that people on the street were watching him.

I must take an alternate route to the Tomiju's location. He didn't want anyone seeing him.

Hiroto ran off into the rain-slicked night.

After sufficient time had passed for the crowd to scatter. Kaen, Hiroto's AI, had found the same staircase that Tomiju and her gigantic companion had used earlier that afternoon. Hiroto descended the steps and was greeted by a rusty-looking door. Hiroto tried to open it, but it was locked. He removed a small leather case from an inside jacket pocket and pulled out some lockpicks. The rain started coming down in sheets; the sound was almost deafening. After a minute or two of fumbling with the lockpicks, he tried another tactic: kicking the door next to the lock. The door flung itself open so violently that hit the inside wall. Hiroto entered the dimly lit building.

"Who goes there? Is that you, Riku?" a man's voice said.

Hiroto waited a moment for his visor to adjust to the darkened room. He changed the visor mode to infrared. He saw two humanoid-looking sources of heat. One came from the voice, but another was far in the distance. Hiroto took evasive action. He removed his katana and assumed a fighting stance as the source of the voice moved closer. He was about to strike when something unexpected happened. An image of a man entered the virtual space of his visor, and a system warning message filled his vision:

It appears that you are a victim of a side-channel visor

attack. The visor's sensory functions have been compromised. Please take your visor to an authorized repair center. Proceed with caution.

How is that possible? Hiroto thought.

"I can see you, fucker, now die!" the man said.

Hiroto's visor crackled. He smelled the foul ozone smell as the visor short-circuited. Something seared into his temples; it felt like hot wax on his skin.

"Argh, it burns!" Hiroto screamed.

The man laughed. "I gotcha now, asshole. I'm going to enjoy this!"

The last image that Hiroto saw as he removed the visor was the man charging toward him. He flung the visor in the man's direction. It struck the man in the chest and fell to the floor.

"You've got to be kidding me!" the man said. "Is that all you have? This is too easy,"

Hiroto didn't need sight to guide his weapon to its destiny; the katana was an extension of himself. In one swift motion, he controlled the blade in an arcing motion—not in the area the man was in, but rather the anticipated position that Hiroto had calculated based on the man's voice and movement. Hiroto was not a cyborg, but he had trained with this katana his entire life. He would often train blindfolded just in case he lost the use of his eyes during a fight. The man screamed as he sliced into him with the blade. The man didn't provide any resistance; it was like Hiroto was attacking a scarecrow. The room suddenly illuminated, and Hiroto had to shield his eyes. Blinded by the luminescence, Hiroto could barely see anything, but he was able to make out at least two shapes moving toward him. The man who he had sliced open performed a clumsy stumbling motion as he attempted to charge.

What the hell is going on? Hiroto thought with panic.

As Hiroto's eyes adjusted to the light, he noticed the man

he'd sliced was disconnecting his ruined arm as if it were a glove. As he replaced it, Hiroto thought he heard a clicking sound.

"That's impossible!" Hiroto said.

"I'm trading up, boyo," the man said as he laughed.

His new appendage was larger and looked out of proportion to the rest of the man's body. It looked like the man's replaced arm was twice as long, and three times wider. Hiroto dodged as the man threw a punch.

"Who—what are you?" Hiroto asked.

"I'm just a bloke with some great enhancements, but I go by Luke. The boss needs someone with your skills—you will make a fine specimen, once you are conditioned."

Hiroto had to sidestep to avoid two more blows in rapid succession. Although Luke's new arm was slow and could be avoided, it wasn't defenseless. Several snake-like tendrils shot out of the arm when it got close to Hiroto. He sensed the man's companion, a lanky fellow, was close. Hiroto didn't know what ability he had, but if it was anything like Luke's, he was screwed.

I need to go on the offensive, and soon.

Hiroto reached for the utility pack he carried on missions; it was lightweight and attached easily to his belt. He grasped a cylinder about the size of a cigarette lighter. He squeezed it, then threw it toward the nearest blurry shape and covered his ears. It exploded, and shrill screams of pain emanated from the men as they writhed on the floor. Hiroto was about to retreat when a flame singed the hairs of his eyebrows. Apparently the other man's talent was shooting fire from his hands.

Enough of this shit.

Hiroto chopped both of the lanky man's hands off at the wrist. The man screamed, but not in pain; it sounded like frustration.

"You will not get off that easy," the lanky man said.

Before Hiroto could react, some substance resembling lava oozed out of the man's stumps. He tried flailing about, desperate to try and use the molten lava material to defend himself. Hiroto responded by decapitating the man.

"You're going to pay for that," Luke said as he aimed his long arm at Hiroto.

Moments later, a half dozen giant, worm-like creatures shot out of the thing that was supposed to be an arm. Hiroto deflected many of them with his katana, but they appeared to have a mind of their own. The snake-like creatures slithered toward Hiroto and started snapping and biting him; it was like getting dozens of paper cuts at the same time. Luke howled with laughter.

"I told you we were special," Luke said.

Hiroto ran past the man, then found himself in a hallway. He navigated the corridor until he entered a darkened room with stacks of boxes. Although the room was dark, it wasn't pitch-black, and he could navigate it well enough. He hid behind a stack of boxes. He found the first-aid ointment in his utility belt and covered his wounds with the sticky substance. As soon as the pain subsided, he tried slowing his breathing so that he could think of his next moves.

"There you are," Luke said.

Hiroto looked in his direction; Luke entered from the far side of the room, not the way Hiroto entered. Hiroto got into another fighting stance, and then readied himself. Luke was fast, but the fight must have taken its toll on Luke too, since he fell as he tried slinging his arm for another attack. Hiroto charged and kicked the man in the face. Luke fell backward in a heap, and then Hiroto made his escape through the open door Luke had entered through.

Treeka awoke in a dark place that reeked of decay. She couldn't focus her eyes and felt drained.

"Take him to the Belmont lab," a man's voice said.

That sounds like the doctor.

"What implants do I need, doctor?" another familiar voice replied.

That's the kid known as Riku. Are they talking about Junior?

Treeka's legs felt rubbery and were starting to get numb. She realized she was pinned vertically against a wall. Treeka tested her restraints, but she could barely move her wrists, let alone force her way out of them. Normally her enhanced cyborg strength would allow her to break them, but she felt too weak to do so. Her teeth chattered.

So cold.

She heard distant screams; they sounded both male and female and seemed to be echoing from another location.

Is that Junior?

"Eliza, are you there?" Treeka asked.

Treeka couldn't remember the last time she communicated with her AI; it must have been days ago. But she couldn't remember. Her vision continued to clear.

Where am I? This place smells like a sewer.

She could make out some basic shapes in the dim light. She appeared to be in a circular shaped room made out of concrete and metal. More screams and moans emanated from further away. It was difficult for Treeka to pinpoint the direction due to the acoustics of whatever chamber of horrors she was in. Then she heard footsteps.

Dr. Sylvester entered the room. He was wearing a white lab coat with blood spattered on it. He looked like someone who worked in a slaughterhouse. He removed his blood-stained gloves, then applied a clear gel substance to his hands. Moments later, he removed something from his pocket.

"Hello, Treeka. I'm sure you can use some of this," the doctor said.

The doctor held out a nutrition cartridge. Her heart fluttered at the sight of it. She licked her lips.

"Yes, I can see you want it—*need* it." The doctor smiled. "I will give it to you, and if you're anything like your sister, then you should recover in minutes."

"Meeka's here?"

The doctor let out a sinister chuckle; he sounded like a madman to Treeka.

"Oh, yes. She's been keeping me company. It gets lonely down here, and it's been a long time since a woman took care of my needs."

"What do you want from me?"

"To cooperate, of course. I'm working toward a plan, but I need your help in achieving it. Your sister has agreed to help me, and so should you."

"Last time I saw my sister, she was dead," Treeka said.

"She was when Riku found her, and the human tissue was just beginning to decay. I had to revitalize the important parts of her and cut away the dead parts."

"I want to see her."

"And you will, but I need you to answer one question."

Treeka nodded, but even that small gesture took too much effort.

"Ask," she said, "and I will answer if I can."

"How much do you know about your creator?"

"Dr. Ash? She's no longer human—she's a computer now."

"Fascinating." The doctor paced around the room before

stopping mere inches from Treeka's face. "Is she connected to an AI?"

Treeka furrowed her brow in concentration. She remembered Dr. Ash talking about an AI, but she couldn't remember any details.

"I remember something about an AI," she replied. "I do not know any details."

Dr. Sylvester showed a picture of Nozomi to Treeka. "Do you know her?"

"I do, and when I get out of here, she's as good as dead."

"Why do you have such a grievance with this one?"

"She was responsible for my sister's death. Nozomi traded us for Dr. Ash's body. I don't think Dr. Ash knew about it—she would not approve."

"Yes, I know the type."

Dr. Sylvester reached out and caressed Treeka's face. Then he took a blade from his pocket and cut the clothes off her body. He rubbed his hands all over her. Treeka recoiled at the man's touch. She tried pulling away, but the doctor was too strong. The doctor continued to glide his hands upon every inch of her body. He got closer; his face was centimeters away from her neck. He kissed it. The scratchiness of his whiskers and the acrid odor of his sweat was almost too much to bear. She bit into his cheek. He pushed her head into the wall with his palm.

"Why do you insist on spoiling the mood? You are a bad girl who needs to be punished," the doctor said.

The next moments were a blur, but she reminded herself to stay strong for Meeka. Her restraints bit into her wrists as the motions of the doctor's lust became more intense. He moved one of her legs, allowing access to her more private areas. He thrust against her for a moment, then convulsed. Her naked body slammed against the cold concrete wall. She retested the restraints as the doctor groaned on.

Ooh . . . how I want this man to suffer.

He stopped for a long moment. He rested his sweaty head on her bare shoulder. His breathing slowed, and then he slowly backed away. The doctor's eyes remained closed for a long moment; he appeared to be controlling his breathing.

Yes, enjoy yourself. I intend to feed your entrails to you later. What kind of sicko pleasures himself fully clothed?

When it was over, the doctor said, "Let's get you to your room."

He removed the restraints, and Treeka dropped to the floor in a heap. Her vision blurred as she tried to focus on the doctor, but all she saw was the vague shape of a man.

"Welcome home, my dear."

CHAPTER 10

THE DOCTOR LED Treeka through a maze of narrow passages filled with pipes, loose wiring, and trash. She heard desperate sounds of people that seemed to echo from everywhere at once. Some corridors were wet as condensation formed on pipes and dripped onto the ground. Occasionally they passed people sitting or just lying on the ground. They were all wearing similar hospital gowns. Treeka's enhanced cybernetic vision filled with an urgent-looking message:

Nutrient levels dangerously low, less than ten percent. Non-essential systems offline.

Treeka's AI was offline, but her built-in cybernetic circuitry informed her of such things in extreme emergency situations. She didn't know how much she depended on her AI until she couldn't use it. One of the features she used was the passive recording feature, which allowed her to playback experiences for further study. This was helpful in dangerous situations with many enemies, as she could pick up clues in her peripheral vision as she rolled the footage back in real-time.

"You will stay here," the doctor said.

He pointed to a darkened room near the end of the hall, which didn't seem to have any other exits.

"Need food, shutting down," Treeka said.

"Oh, I'm sorry my dear," the doctor replied. "I will feed you soon, but I have an urgent matter to attend to."

Treeka shuffled into the room. Basic functions like walking were becoming difficult. She perked up when she spotted the clean bed and an oversized bottle of water on a nightstand. She collapsed on the bed. Treeka couldn't remember the last time she'd had a good night's rest. The doctor started saying something, but she couldn't make out the words. Sleep took her in seconds.

Treeka awoke to a darkened room. She tried activating her cybernetic system overlay. She tapped her right temple three times. Nothing happened.

What happened to my interface? Treeka thought.

Her mouth was as dry as a desert. She seized the bottle of water and drank. A wave of relief washed over her as she hydrated herself. She reached for the metal plate covering the left side of her torso. She found the indentation and opened the access panel that contained her nutrition cartridge. To her surprise, the cartridge was back. She ejected it and checked the nutrient level. The glass on the side of the cartridge allowed her to measure the contents at a glance. It was full.

The doctor must have refilled it.

The color was different, however; normally her nutrient fluid was a pinkish color. The color of her fluid levels resembled an inky color.

She replaced the cartridge and examined the room. It was about ten feet long and four feet wide. A single bed and a small table were the only furnishings.

Except for my offline AI and systems interface, I feel a lot better. That doctor must have disabled my cybernetic interface somehow.

The door to the room opened, and a man in his early twenties appeared. He was short, clean-shaven, and had black hair. He looked Japanese and reminded her of a classmate she'd once known. He was holding a stack of garments.

"You're awake," the man said.

He set the clothes on the foot of the bed, then turned to leave. His eyes diverted away from her. It was like he was avoiding her nakedness.

"Wait!" Treeka said.

The man stopped.

"I'm not supposed to be in your room alone," he said. "But I wanted to make sure you had something to wear."

"Is there another woman like me here?"

The man looked out into the hallway, then closed the door quietly.

"I remember you from before—you're Riku, right?" Treeka asked.

"Yes, and there is another woman. But I can't talk now," he said as he left the room.

He looks nervous—like we're being watched.

Treeka looked through the pile of clothes. The man had brought her an outfit comprised of a blouse, sweatpants, panties, socks, and shoes. As she got dressed, she examined the room for cameras or listening devices. If she were being watched, she didn't want her captors to know she suspected anything. She needed to catch them by surprise.

Nozomi agreed to meet Dr. Sylvester at the backdoor alley entrance of the underground. Groups of people clustered themselves in various areas around the manhole cover that would grant her access. She thought about letting Beatrice take over to remove the cover again but thought better of it.

I thought I knew every inch of my body and what my capabilities and limitations were. I guess I have more to learn. I'm not letting anyone take over any part of me again, especially not an AI.

As she stared at the manhole cover, she was transported back to an earlier time. Someone was removing a blindfold from her eyes. Moments later, a thin, older-looking man with gray hair was staring down at her. He was wearing an elegant black suit with a yellow happy face button with crossed-out eyes, which seemed to be out of place on the expensive-looking suit. He was smoking a cigarette and blew the smoke toward her. Nozomi covered her mouth—not because of the smoke, but because she was disgusted with this man: the man who had hurt her brother.

"Bring her to me," the man in the suit said.

Another younger man took her by the arm and pulled her up, then pushed her toward the older man with the suit.

"Before we begin, I need to ask you a question, and I want your honest answer. Do you understand what you have agreed to?" The older man asked.

Nozomi nodded.

"I need a verbal response."

"Yes. You want me to . . . hurt you?" Nozomi said, hesitantly.

The older man smiled.

"Something like that, but not in a way that you may think. I'm going to teach you the art of extracting pleasure from the pain from others. If I'm correct about you, I think you will enjoy it," the older man said.

"Then my brother will be released?"

"You have my word."

Nozomi was so deep in thought she didn't hear the manhole cover move. She looked to see the young man she had previously followed crawling out of the sewer.

"Dr. Sylvester sent me," the young man asked. "Are you ready?"

Nozomi nodded. "Do you work for the doctor?" she asked.

"Yes, I take care of many technical tasks and physical security," the young man said.

"What's your name?"

"My name is Riku. Now come, we don't have a lot of time."

He took off one of his gloves, revealing a metal hand. He performed the same trick that Beatrice had used with her hand. The manhole cover moved effortlessly. He removed a key from a pocket, reached in, and unlocked a panel that was built into a wall. Then she heard a clicking sound, and the darkness illuminated.

"This is so you can see where you're going. There are areas where you might get hurt in the dark," Riku said.

That would have been nice to know about when I was delving in the dark earlier.

Nozomi descended into the underworld. Several ancient-looking lights were mounted on the walls. Viewing the area while illuminated changed her perception of the place. The tunnel was larger than it looked. Metal scaffolding was set up throughout the underground. Nozomi spotted many areas where she could have fallen to her death if she had taken a wrong step.

"This way," Riku said, pointing to another ladder.

Nozomi followed Riku through several areas. He took a different route then she remembered taking the last time.

"Isn't there a more direct path?" Nozomi asked.

"Not if you want to avoid the gangs that roam these tunnels. Besides, we are almost there."

Riku's detour brought them to a grating far above a white door she recognized as the entrance to the doctor's lab. She estimated it was about a thirty-foot drop to the next level. He removed the grate, then reached out and grabbed on to a pipe that was attached to a nearby wall.

"Follow me," he said. "There's a path. It's hard to see, but I know the way."

Riku scuttled along the pipe until he reached another platform. Nozomi continued to follow Riku through a maze of soggy cardboard, trash, and other debris before emerging through a nondescript metal door. She hadn't noticed this door before.

This place must have dozens of forgotten passages.

Riku pressed on a loose brick near the lab's entrance. It popped out, and a mechanical lock with six numbers appeared. He attempted to hide the digits on the keypad as he pushed in the corrected combination. A popping noise emitted as the door unlocked. With some effort, Riku got the door open. She recognized the dingy concrete stairwell. A strong musty odor hit Nozomi as she entered.

Dr. Sylvester met them in the familiar hallway.

"Welcome, I'm happy to see you back so soon," Dr. Sylvester said.

"I have a proposal for you," Nozomi said.

"Let's talk in my office. Riku, please secure the facility and meet us in the lab," Dr. Sylvester said.

Nozomi followed the doctor to the end of the long hallway. A red door appeared at the end of the hall, standing in stark contrast to the white surrounding it.

The hall must curve in a downward direction. Or it's an optical illusion, Nozomi thought.

Dr. Sylvester removed a massive key from his coat pocket and opened the red door.

A faint light was visible from above. The area the doctor was taking her through resembled a maintenance shaft more than a path to an office, but she didn't question the route. After climbing a series of ladders, she followed the doctor along a narrow passage. The passage stopped at another door. He opened it. Bright light shone onto the path, and she followed him into the light.

After another jaunt up several flights of stairs, he opened the door to a large area with several windows. She could see a secluded, tree-lined street outside. Another door was visible on the other side of the room. There was a single desk and a lamp, and an old beige computer with an ancient cathode-ray tube (CRT) monitor resting on the computer casing took up half the desk. The keyboard looked so dirty that she could barely make out some of the letters. The doctor fetched a folding chair from a nearby closet.

"So, what do you have for me?" Dr. Sylvester asked.

"I've spoken to my creator, and she has agreed to help you perfect the skin if you help us with perfecting the construction of the data core technology," Nozomi said.

"That trade seems reasonable. I have cleared some lab space for your creator. When will we be able to meet in person?"

"Now," Nozomi replied. "I have a message for you."

Nozomi accessed her enhanced AR interface.

"Beatrice, can you replay the message for the good doctor?" Nozomi said.

Moments later, a full-color image of Dr. Ash appeared, floating in mid-air. She was wearing a white lab coat that matched her white hair. The image was projected from Nozomi's left eye. Dr. Ash spoke in a British accent through Nozomi's mouth.

"Hello, Dr. Sylvester. I'm Dr. Elizabeth Ash. Sorry I can't be there in person, but I hope we can meet someday soon. For now, Nozomi will be our proxy. I look forward to our continued collaboration," Dr. Ash said through Nozomi.

The image of Dr. Ash faded.

"I'm very familiar with Dr. Ash's work, but I did not know how advanced her experiments had become," Dr. Sylvester said to Nozomi. "She stopped publishing papers on her work more than twenty years ago."

He's thorough.

"Are you a doctor too?" Dr. Sylvester asked.

"No, my talents lie in other areas. She is the best geneticist on the planet," Nozomi said.

"When do you think we can get started?"

"Immediately," Nozomi said.

She reached into the space between her breasts and produced a small flash drive. "I assume this dinosaur of a computer can read this?"

Dr. Sylvester took the flash drive from Nozomi, then opened a drawer from his desk and took out a small tablet. After a moment, the information was transferred onto it. He opened the files, and a three-dimensional image of applying the synthetic skin appeared with detailed files on how to make it.

"It looks like I will need to get some upgrades before I can make use of the files. Thank you for delivering it personally," Dr. Sylvester said.

Nozomi nodded.

"If you have a modern tablet, what do you need the old computer for?" she asked.

"It has old research notes and other information I cannot

transfer. I keep it around in case I need to access the older information," Dr. Sylvester explained.

"I've shown you mine—now how about yours?" Nozomi said teasingly.

Dr. Sylvester smiled. "Of course. It's in the lab —follow me."

Nozomi followed the doctor through another door leading from the office. This area looked different from their previous trek.

"Where are we going?" Nozomi asked.

"I'm taking you to the lab—think of it as a shortcut," Dr. Sylvester said.

The doctor led her through several labyrinthine passages and tunnels. Instead of entering the white corridor, she found herself in a dank, dark hallway. He stopped briefly at a black metal door. Then the doctor took out a pair of black gloves and put them on before opening the door.

Water splashed underfoot as they stepped through the threshold and into a small oval-shaped room. On the far side of the room, another smaller door appeared. The doctor opened it and had to duck under the low threshold. The interior reminded Nozomi of the inside of an old battleship she had visited as a girl. The doctor appeared to be fiddling with something on the other side of the open door. Then he turned and smiled at her before grasping the handle of a rod-shaped object and lowering it into position.

What's he doing?

Before Nozomi could complete the thought, an electric shock coursed through her as the wet chamber conducted the electricity into her body. She fell to her knees, then screamed in agony. A warning message filled her vision:

Warning, your circuits have suffered a massive power surge. Synapses and pain receptors have been disabled to prevent further damage to the subsystem. You have thirty seconds before the system is permanently damaged.

The electric shock only lasted a few seconds, but it felt like an eternity. Nozomi saw Dr. Sylvester pull up the lever making additional adjustments to whatever controls he was trying to use. His movements became erratic and hurried. He turned some kind of dial on a nearby panel, then tried pulling the lever again, but it seemed stuck. Nozomi removed a small knife from her belt and threw it at the doctor, but it hit the doorframe instead.

The doctor is trying to kill me . . . need to get out of . . . water.

Nozomi tried going back the way she had come. She was almost at the door when a more intense electrical shock jolted her. She grasped the doorframe and pulled herself forward. Her skin was turning black in some places, mainly in areas where it touched the electrified water.

System Message:
System shutdown in progress to prevent further damage.
She collapsed on the floor as the world went dark.

Unidentified Building, subbasement, Upper West Side, New York

The open door lead to a dark, crumbling concrete staircase that looked like it had been constructed more than a hundred years ago. Chunks of concrete were missing from many stairs, and metal was visible in the chipped areas. Hiroto scrambled down the stairs as quickly as he dared.

"There you are," Luke said as he pursued.

Hiroto looked back and noticed an average-looking man with a gigantic left hand; Hiroto didn't know how he could keep the hand elevated.

These cybernetic augmentations are unreal. I've never seen anything like it.

The bottom of the stairs led to another long passageway that led into complete darkness. Hiroto trotted through, hoping he wouldn't run into any unseen pit or other danger. He did not know where this passage would take him, but he didn't relish fighting Luke again. After about five minutes of jogging through the underground tunnel, something hit his body so hard that it knocked him to the floor. Hiroto leaped back onto his feet in one motion, shook off the blow, and readied his katana. But nothing else happened.

Did I just run into a wall?

Hiroto tapped his smartwatch, and it lit up the area with a soft glow. Luke's distant shambling could be heard, echoing through the hall.

It is a wall. I'm lucky I didn't get hit in the head. I'd better get the hell out of here before Luke catches up.

Hiroto noticed a metal grating built into the wall. He wiggled it, and it fell to the ground. The echo of the commotion would carry, but he knew he needed to escape. He entered the space the grate covered; it provided just enough room for Hiroto to crawl though. However, there was nothing to grasp— no handholds or anything, just metal walls. He tried traversing using his arms, but after a moment he knew he needed to try something else.

"I'm coming for you," Luke said.

The menacing voice of the elongated freak sounded much closer now; it was practically on top of him.

I need to do something, quick . . . the knife!

Hiroto carried a small knife for fighting in confined areas. He removed the knife, then continued crawling deeper into the shaft. With a free hand, he tested the metal shaft's wall. In areas where it flexed, Hiroto stabbed his knife, then pulled himself deeper into the shaft. Hiroto heard a clanking sound behind him, along with some curses. He looked back to find the enormous arm trying to reach for him, but Luke appeared to be stuck. Hiroto resumed his shaft crawl, and while he was sure Luke couldn't catch him, he kept moving.

Eventually, Hiroto reached another grating. A faint glow was visible beyond. When he was satisfied no one was in the immediate area, he punched the grate. Pain shot through his hands as though he'd punched a brick wall. Using the flashlight function of his watch, he examined the grating. It appeared to be integrated with the wall. He checked the edges. A small opening about the size of a fifty-cent piece was visible on the edge of the grate. He started chipping away at it with the knife. Moments later the wall crumbled, and large pieces fell toward his face. Hiroto choked on the dust his activity had caused, but he kept working at it until he had enough room to put his arm through. He reached through the opening, feeling for a lever or something to open the grate. Instead, the grating popped out of the wall like a nail being driven through a soft piece of wood. Before he could react, two sets of hands pulled him from the wall as if he weighed nothing. Hiroto noticed he was on a catwalk with two other men. The room he was pulled into was massive; it looked like an underground warehouse with a trench running through it.

"Look what we have here, Jonny," a man's voice said.

The men were enormous. The man known as Jonny was at least six feet tall, and his arms were massive, with biceps as big as Hiroto's hips. The other man seemed to be of normal proportions for a human, but he also seemed to have the strength of many.

"Oh my, the doctor will be so pleased. Blake, do you think he might even give us a bonus?" Jonny said.

Hiroto thrust the knife toward Jonny. Jonny blocked the

strike, with his forearm taking most of the impact. The man let out a shrill scream that echoed throughout the chamber. Despite the wound, Jonny held on to Hiroto. He pulled the blade out of his arm, then tried to stab Hiroto, who responded by punching him in his injured bicep. Jonny dropped Hiroto, but he still had the knife. Jonny flailed the knife in Hiroto's direction, who dodged the blows and kicked the man in the groin. The big man dropped the knife. Blake reached for it, but Hiroto was faster. In one fluid motion, he grabbed the weapon and thrust it into the big man's leg.

"Argh, you bastard," Jonny said.

The other man known as Blake struck Hiroto on the back of his head; it felt like a car had hit him. Hiroto's vision blurred as the pummeling continued. He got his blade into position. With a newfound burst of strength, Hiroto plunged it into Blake's chest. Blood gushed from the wound, and the man stumbled back into a railing.

Hiroto got a better look at the platform. It was about two dozen feet off the ground, and a staircase led down. Then Jonny charged Hiroto, who drew his katana just as the man closed the gap. Hiroto plunged the sword into the man's stomach. Blood oozed from the gaping wound and the man's mouth.

"Die!" Hiroto said.

As Jonny collapsed, he grabbed Hiroto by the shirt so hard that he went down with him. Hiroto pushed Jonny over to his side and watched him bleed out. Blake was nearby, slumped over and clutching his chest. He whimpered as his lifeblood escaped. Exhausted and hurt, Hiroto sat on the platform watching the men die. He took no pleasure in their deaths—he just wanted to complete his mission. Tomiju was depending on him.

He felt his strength flag, but he forced himself to keep going. He removed his utility belt, then took out a thick, oversized, pen-like device and plunged it into his chest. A jolt of adrenaline coursed through his system, renewing his energy.

Hiroto took stock of his situation. All the adversaries he'd encountered so far were stronger than him, but he had the advantage of speed and a mastery of his katana. As he reflected, he heard the sounds of agonized misery, which seemed to be coming from everywhere at once.

Am I in hell?

After a moment, he headed toward the sounds that emanated throughout the halls. He was almost at the end of the catwalk when he heard a door open; it was difficult to tell where the sound had come from due to the cavernous nature of the room, but he got out of sight, ducking into a side room next to a staircase leading down. He hid behind some moldy crates but kept the catwalk in plain view through an open doorway.

"I sawz the fight from below," a man's voice said.

Hiroto could hardly make out the words; it sounded like babble. Moments later, a man appeared, and he was wearing what appeared to be some sort of straitjacket. A young Asian man followed him. After what seemed like an eternity, the harnessed man ran past the open door. Hiroto waited another moment before leaving the safety of his hideout. He couldn't risk waiting there much longer; he had to get to the stairs.

As he left the room, he heard a gasp. He turned to see the man in the straitjacket. The man opened his mouth, and he looked like he was going to scream, but only a croaking sound came out. Hiroto put a finger over his lips. The man complied. Hiroto had no wish to harm the man, especially since he didn't seem to be in his right mind; there would be no honor in that. He descended the stairs two at a time, then bolted out of the expansive room as soon as his feet hit the ground.

Dr. Sylvester Javitts consulted his tablet, then scribbled some calculations into a legal-sized tablet. His phone chirped. It was Riku.

"What is it?" the doctor asked in an annoyed tone.

"We have an intruder in the Belmont tunnels," Riku said.

"Send Jonny and Blake to handle the situation."

"We did, they're dead. Whoever is attacking us is a threat we are not equipped to handle."

"Take Treeka and her sister and meet me at the safe house. I will have a surprise waiting for our intruder."

The doctor turned off the tablet, then headed for his secret lab. The underground passages he had inherited from a city project partitioned off most of the area between two train stations. The area was ideal for his operations since no one knew of its existence. The urban explorers who were unfortunate enough to discover his hidden corner would eventually join the good doctor's growing legion of cybernetic soldiers.

"Stop," a male voice said.

Dr. Sylvester turned toward the voice. An Asian man of medium build, dressed in black, revealed himself from behind a series of conduits. He held his samurai sword mere inches from the doctor's face.

"It takes a true master to sneak up on a man who is used to hiding in the shadows," the doctor said.

The man with the sword stood there, unwavering.

"I can help you," the doctor urged.

"Yes, I believe you can. Give me Tomiju and Misato, and I will be on my way."

"Who?"

"Don't play dumb—the cyborgs that you stole."

"I have not stolen anything."

The samurai raised the sword to Dr. Sylvester's neck, and a drop of blood dripped on the doctor's collar.

"I don't believe you. Now lead me to them," the samurai said, kicking the doctor into motion.

The doctor led the samurai through a series of passages before stopping at a dead end.

"She's in there," the doctor said, pointing to a door.

"Open it and enter."

The doctor did as the samurai asked.

The sounds of a crying female came from a darkened room. The samurai entered the room to find a woman, who was about twenty, lying naked on a soiled bed. She was in a fetal position, holding some kind of stuffed animal. She appeared to be malnourished and dirty.

"Tomiju, I'm here to take you to your father," the samurai said as he put a comforting hand on her shoulder.

The doctor reached into his pocket as slowly as he dared. The samurai sensed the movement, and before the doctor could react, he had his sword pointed at his chest.

"No sudden movements," the samurai said.

The doctor raised his hands.

"What's that in your hands?"

"It's my earplugs," the doctor replied. "The acoustics in this place give me vertigo. I feel a spell coming on, and I don't wish to pass out. I would like to put them in—with your permission, of course."

The samurai nodded, and then the doctor put the earplugs in.

The woman moaned and turned to face the samurai. The whites in her eyes were solid black, and the irises were a dull gray color; they looked lifeless. Then the woman screamed like a banshee. The piercing attack registered at least one-hundred and twenty decibels on the samurai's watch. The sound was paralyzing in the enclosed area. He gave in, covering his ears and falling to his knees. His sword fell to the floor. The doctor took it and held it to the samurai's neck. Moments later, the screeching stopped. The doctor removed the earplugs with one hand and held the sword with the other.

"As a trained killer, you should know better," the doctor said.

The samurai's ears were bleeding.

"Let me look at your injury." The doctor examined the samurai. "You will live, but you will be uncomfortable for a long time."

Moments later, two men entered the room. One of the men was skinny, and he was shaking; his red mohawk made him look like a kid's toy. The other man was massive and looked like a mobster. His stony face and demeanor gave anyone the impression that if anyone crossed him, they would be six feet under.

"We heard the siren's wail. Is he the intruder?" the skinny man asked, pointing to the samurai.

The doctor smiled. "Perceptive as ever, Salvatore."

The mobster-like man punched the samurai in the gut, who doubled over in pain. Then the giant restrained the samurai with a pair of zip ties.

"Easy, Grumpie, he's been through a lot," the doctor said. "I admire how far he got into my inner sanctum. Treat him with more respect, please."

The enormous man shrugged, then said, "Elimination or reeducation?"

"Hmmm," Dr. Sylvester considered, "I do think he would make an excellent addition to the program. And we do need more recruits, but I'm worried he might be too powerful." The doctor rubbed at his unshaven whiskers. "What do you two think?"

The two men gave each other a look; it was rare the doctor asked them for their opinion. Salvatore flinched involuntarily. "Ooh, I would love to have some fun with this one. We could tie him up and poke him. Or stuff him with candy and hit him like a pinata. Or . . ." The man twitched again. He seemed to get frustrated, and then he slapped himself a few times. He shook his head, as if to clear it before speaking again. "If reeducation doesn't work, we can still have our fun . . . later."

"Let's reeducate him—he might be good ally," Grumpie said.

"Excellent, take him to the indoctrination chamber," the doctor said.

The giant threw the samurai over his shoulders, then left the room. Salvatore followed close behind.

CHAPTER 11

FIFTEEN MINUTES **earlier**

Treeka lay on the bed, staring at the ceiling. It had been hours since someone had checked in on her. She didn't find any cameras or listening devices in the room but concluded her ability to check on such things was compromised without the use of her full cybernetic interface. A knocking at the door broke her concentration.

As she sat up, the door opened; it was the young man who didn't want to look at her naked.

There is something odd about this man.

"We have to go," the man said.

"Wait, I'm still a little confused," Treeka replied. "Who are you again?"

"I'm Riku. The doctor has asked that I ensure your safety. We are going to a safer location."

Now that I feel so much better, I might have a chance to escape.

"Just us, or will the doctor be there?"

Riku looked confused.

"I don't much care for the doctor, and someone has interfered with my cybernetic interface—I cannot access my menus," Treeka explained.

"I suppose the doctor will be there, but he won't arrive for a while."

"Can you fix my interface?"

"I didn't know it could be disabled. Dr. Sylvester must have done it for a reason."

"Can you check on it for me?"

"I will check on it after we leave here—now come, we need to hurry."

Treeka leaped off the bed. She marveled to herself how normal she felt again.

"What happened to Junior?" Treeka asked.

Riku flinched a little.

"I'm not sure, but he's probably at the Belmont."

"Is that hotel the doctor mentioned when you captured us?"

Riku looked toward the floor like he'd spotted something interesting.

"It's a place—"

A screeching noise reverberated throughout the room. Treeka and Riku covered their ears; the sound was paralyzing. After a moment, Riku reached for something in his pocket. He put earplugs in both of his ears. He rummaged through his pack and found another pair for Treeka. After she put them in, he urged her to leave.

Riku held Treeka's hand and guided her through the maze of passages and narrow corridors. Treeka was having a hard time keeping track of where they were without her cybernetic interface. She noticed several people writhing on the floor covering their ears; some looked enhanced, while others did not. They all were in pain.

After following Riku for what seemed like hours, he

stopped at a nondescript door at the end of a corridor. The screeching noise had stopped, so Riku urged her to remove her earplugs. She put them in a pocket.

"Someone close to you is behind that door," Riku said as he opened the door.

She looked up to see Meeka lying on a bed with two pillows over her ears. The sight would have been comical in other circumstances.

"Treeka!" Meeka said.

Treeka ran to her sister and hugged her for several long moments. Meeka responded with a coy look that eventually turned into a smirk that Treeka knew well.

That's the same look you would give father when you were caught or up to no good. What are you up to, sister?

"How long . . . have you been awake?" Treeka asked.

"The doctor revived me, but if it had not been for this young man, I would still be lying in the gutter," Meeka said.

There was something different about Meeka's tone, and Treeka knew that tone well; it meant that Meeka wanted to show her savior a good time. Riku blushed, then looked away.

It looks like Meeka has been showing Riku her gratitude already.

"It's not safe here, Meeka," Treeka told her. "I think you need to come with us."

"Is Sylvester coming? I miss assisting him," Meeka said.

Treeka flushed as she thought of the doctor seducing her sister.

What? This is not the Meeka I know. If I didn't know any better, I think that Meeka likes the doctor.

"What . . . assistance have you been providing, sister?" Treeka asked.

"Besides the sex?" Meeka laughed. "That part was unremarkable—I don't think the man knows how to treat a woman—but I've been helping him in other ways."

Treeka urged Meeka to continue; she was interested in learning what her relationship with the doctor was.

"He has been reeducating people," Meeka said. "He has a special chamber he puts people in. He also injects them with drugs and blasts them with all kinds of images, shrill music, and voices. It's fun to help."

"It sounds like he's torturing and brainwashing people," Treeka said.

"It's more than that, big sister. It's like he's changing them mentally before the augmentations."

"What kind of augmentation?"

"Cybernetics, like us, but way cooler. Some of these guys can shoot fire or electricity. There's this guy named Rick—"

"And you're assisting him? Why?"

Meeka smiled. "Because he's fun. He also promised to fix my face."

Treeka's heart sank as she looked at her sister's ruined face —the result of getting shot by one of Nozomi's cronies.

That's another reason to hate that bitch.

"We need to leave," Riku protested.

"Alright," Meeka said, "but I want to come back and play with Sly—I mean, Sylvester."

She has a pet name for him? Meeka only does that for men she likes.

"It's good to have you back, sister," Meeka said.

The twins followed Riku out of the subterranean maze of dank corridors. They found themselves on an underground train track. A faded sign labeled "Belmont Line" was visible on a wall with an enormous arrow; Riku followed the sign. After what seemed like an eternity, the narrow train tunnel widened to a large, expansive area. A train car with lights shining from it appeared in the center of the room.

"This way," Riku said, pointing to a side door.

"What's in there?" Treeka asked.

"Oh, that's where the meat man is stored," Meeka said.

"Who is this meat man?"

"A few days ago, I helped the doctor get this giant of a man restrained. The usual audiovisual treatment wasn't working for him, so Sly had to do something far more creative."

"Is this man six feet tall, balding, but friendly?"

"That sounds like him."

Treeka ran toward the train car. When she opened the door, a wave of filth that smelled like rotten meat, trash, urine, and vomit assaulted her nostrils. She covered her mouth and looked away for a moment.

"Junior?" she called. She looked into the train car and saw Junior slumped over at the other end.

"You know the meat man, sister?" Meeka asked.

Treeka's eyes filled with tears as she took in Junior's condition. A series of thin wires stretched across the train car and were stapled into Junior's skin. His hands were pulled to either side of his body at awkward angles. He appeared to be bleeding in several places. Treeka gasped as she noticed fingers and other unidentifiable fleshy clumps surrounding Junior; it looked like someone had carved him up with the piano wire.

"What did you do to him?" Treeka asked Meeka.

"Sly was getting angry that he wouldn't accept any of his cybernetic gifts or respond to the training, so he put him here," Meeka replied.

Treeka glared at Riku. "Is this the hotel the doctor spoke so fondly of?"

Riku looked away from her penetrating stare.

"You have feelings for this man?" Meeka said. "I'm so sorry, sister. If I had known—"

"What would you have done?" Treeka yelled. "Your doctor friend is a monster!"

"No, he's not—he brought me back and fed me. He gave me these clothes and everything."

"I'm going to kill him. Are you with me, little sister?"

Meeka hesitated; she seemed conflicted. Treeka took Meeka by the hands and stared into her eyes.

"We are blood, and nobody can come between us. Our bond is too strong. Please tell me you're with me," Treeka pleaded.

"You need to come with me, Meeka. We had a deal," Riku said.

You know I'm with you, big sister, Meeka responded telepathically.

Follow my lead, Treeka said.

Treeka tried to undo the piano wire from Junior's hands, wrists, and other parts of his body. He cried out in pain as she attempted to loosen his bindings. Junior tried to say something; Treeka removed his gag.

"Treeka," he gasped, "leave this place and never return. This doctor is a sick bastard—he will hurt you too."

Tears rolled down Treeka's face. She had not realized how much Junior had meant to her until this moment.

That doctor is going to pay for this.

"You need to stop. You're going to ruin everything," Riku said as he tried pulling Treeka away. She turned and punched Riku in the jaw hard enough to make a nasty cracking sound. He choked, then spit several teeth out. He made an eerie, half-screaming and half-gurgling sound as he spit more teeth out.

Treeka pulled on a piece of wire that was connected to the side of the rail car; the wire made a strange springing sound as it came loose. Riku removed a black box from his pack and pulled a bulky trigger on the device. Electrified wires plunged into Treeka's clothes and skin, and she stiffened and convulsed.

"No, Riku!" Meeka said as she kicked him in the face. He bounced off the wall of the train car, then fell to the floor. Meeka grabbed the stun gun and deactivated it. Treeka collapsed to the floor, panting.

I'm going to kill that little bastard.

A flood of memory assaulted her mind with every negative feeling she'd experienced since being awakened by Dr. Ash. Images of Carmine assaulting her, Jon laughing at her mutilated body, the doctor's sexual assault, Nozomi's betrayal: every emotion was remembered and felt. It was like someone had bottled up her suffering and then unleashed it all at once. She let the white-hot anger envelop her.

Treeka looked at Riku, who was busy trying to open the door to the rail car. She leaped into the air and landed on his back. He let out a frightened scream. Treeka bit into his earlobe. As fresh blood filled her mouth, she basked in the glory of the kill. For a moment she felt like a huntress that had caught her quarry. She spit the severed ear onto the floor. Riku was paralyzed with fear.

"Now you will die," Treeka said, wiping the blood from her mouth.

Riku tried to flee once more, but Treeka kicked him from behind, and he stumbled and fell. She resumed kicking his face until nothing but a bloody pulp remained. Treeka stared at the goo that had been Riku. Not long ago her own actions would have horrified her, but now she just looked at Riku like a bug that needed to be exterminated. She felt no remorse or pity about taking his life.

"Bye-bye, Riku. It was almost fun," Meeka said, chuckling.

"Find something to help free Junior," Treeka said.

Meeka gave her sister a wary look, but she obeyed without question.

"Stop! Treeka, save yourself," Junior said in a gasp.

Treeka contemplated his predicament; Junior was correct. She examined the positioning of the wires. They were embedded in every portion of his enormous body. She feared that removing the wires would kill him.

It's better to end his suffering now, she thought sadly.

"You've done nothing but help me, I can't let you go," Treeka said.

"Please make the pain stop," Junior pleaded.

Junior coughed up some sort of bloody blob; Treeka couldn't identify what it was. Then Junior began to sob. Treeka couldn't take it any longer. She searched Riku's body for a weapon and found some sort of gun. It didn't look like any weapon that Treeka had ever seen. She examined it and saw three settings with different intensity levels. She hoped that red was the deadliest of all settings. She moved the lever into position, then fired. An instant later, Junior's head exploded in every direction. She was splattered in gray matter, bone fragments, and copious amounts of blood.

Treeka collapsed and wept, not only for Junior, but for the loss of her humanity. She closed her eyes and was transported to her father's backyard: her favorite place growing up. A young Misato brought her an anpan, her favorite pastry. She took her sister's hand and strode to their favorite spot under an oak tree to eat their snack.

System Message:

Warning: Nonessential functions shutting down to prevent biological systems exhaustion. Core dump immanent.

Blackness enveloped Treeka, and she fell into a dreamless slumber.

Nozomi awoke naked and strapped to a cold table in a circular room. For a moment she didn't have any memory of what had happened to her, and then it all came back in a rush of emotion. The doctor had betrayed her, and she couldn't think of a logical reason why. Her cybernetic interface and AI were unavailable. She couldn't remember the last time she'd felt so alone. She lifted her head to see what damage the electricity had done to her body. Her hands and arms were nearly blackened and torn in many places. Although she felt no physical pain, seeing her body in this manner was distressing. Tears welled in her eyes. It was rare for her to show any emotion, but she repressed those feelings the best she could.

"Are you ready for the operation?" a woman's voice said.

Nozomi looked around the room but saw no one. Then the image of a familiar woman appeared from the corner of the room. Despite missing half of her face, she appeared happy.

"Meeka?" Nozomi said in disbelief.

"Yes, it's me. In the flesh—or should I say, in *your* flesh?"

Meeka laughed as she caressed Nozomi's perfect face. Dr. Sylvester entered the room.

"Hello, Nozomi, I forgot to thank you for the skin formula. I don't have the required equipment, however, and based on my calculations, your dear Dr. Ash has omitted the most important ingredient," Dr. Sylvester said.

"What ingredient?" Nozomi said.

"Since you're not a scientist, I won't bother explaining the details, but rest assured, it's a problem."

"That means I get your skin—isn't that right, Sly?" Meeka said in a playful, childish voice.

Is she going mad? Nozomi wondered.

The doctor gave Nozomi a regretful look. "Your skin is

perfect. Believe me when I say this is going to hurt me more than it will you. I have disabled your pain receptors—you won't feel a thing."

"How in the hell is it going to hurt you? I'm the one getting my face peeled off," Nozomi spat.

"Cutting into your face is like performing surgery on a priceless work of art. It's heart-wrenching for me, so please be quiet, and don't make it any more difficult than it needs to be," the doctor said.

Nozomi flailed back and forth.

"Nurse, I can't work with the patient flopping around like this," Dr. Sylvester said.

Meeka returned wearing a nurse's outfit. She put a mask over Nozomi's face.

"Nighty night, it's sleepy time," Meeka said as she cackled.

Sometime later, Nozomi awoke, and she was in pain. She couldn't remember when or if she'd ever experienced such pain. Her eyes watered. She bit her lip, but it didn't help. Then she screamed. Moments later, Meeka came into view. She gazed upon Nozomi like a woman considering a piece of meat for her dinner.

"Now, I've had enough of this young girl," Meeka said as she gagged Nozomi with a dirty rag.

Nozomi couldn't believe the monstrosity she was looking at: Meeka's natural olive complexion had been patched together using sections of Nozomi's white face. The look was both disturbing and fascinating. Then the doctor emerged from whatever hole he'd been hiding in, removed Nozomi's bandages, and examined her face.

"It's been a few hours since the operation, but I'm happy to report that it was a success," the doctor announced. "I wish to thank you again for your contribution."

Nozomi let out a ragged gasp. Sweat poured from her body because of the trauma. She screamed again.

"Oh, silly me, I forgot to give you something for the pain," the doctor said.

He injected her in the neck with a syringe. Meeka gave the doctor a hug.

"Thank you for the gift, dear," Meeka cooed.

"You're most welcome, dear," the doctor replied.

Nozomi's vision blurred, then faded. The last thing she saw before she blacked out was the doctor and Meeka embracing.

Treeka awoke to the nightmare in the train car. She didn't know how long she slept, but it seemed like a lifetime.

"Meeka?" Treeka said to the empty train car.

She noticed a white leather belt loop sticking out of Riku's pack. To her surprise, it looked like the belt Nozomi always wore. She wriggled it loose from Riku's body, then checked for the knives that Nozomi always had concealed in the belt; they were there, and intact. She strapped them to her arms in case she needed them.

I'm so damned tired of all the pain.

Treeka gazed at Junior's body one last time. She had no more tears to shed, but she said a silent goodbye, then left the train car. She was in a daze. The man who had risked his life to help her escape from one of the most notorious crime lords in New York had been carved up by a mad doctor. It all seemed like a cruel joke.

"Stand down, Treeka, drop the weapon," a man's voice said. She looked in the direction of the voice. It was Dr.

Sylvester, with Meeka by his side. He was holding some kind of shotgun, and it was pointed at Treeka's head. She estimated the distance to be about twenty feet away. She assessed the situation; if he was holding a conventional shotgun, then the pellets would scatter in a wide area, and would not be fatal. She also noticed the shotgun was glowing. If it were anything like Riku's gun, then it had multiple intensity settings. She had no idea how much blasting power it had, but she decided to give it a wide berth.

Treeka dropped the gun she was holding.

"Good choice, sister," Meeka said.

My sister is truly lost.

"What happened to you, sister? You betray me for this— man?" Treeka said in disgust.

Meeka looked away from her sister. She stared at the ground as if she'd found something interesting there. Treeka noticed her sister's face was different; a crude patchwork of skin had replaced the exposed metal. The pigment was several shades lighter than Meeka's natural olive complexion.

"Where did you get the skin, sister?" Treeka asked.

Meeka grinned, and it made the butcher job that much more horrifying to behold.

"Did you know that Sly captured Nozomi?" Meeka said.

"It would be terrible to let her skin go to waste," the doctor said as he caressed Meeka's newly attached skin.

Meeka seemed to purr like an oversized cat. Treeka was speechless.

"Your sister is important to me, so I will give you something that no one gets around here. A choice," Dr. Sylvester said.

"What choice?" Treeka asked.

"I need you to lure Dr. Ash to this location. She has perfected the skin, and I need it to help your sister."

"And if I refuse?"

"Then deactivation is immanent. Your sister can use a twin body to provide her with spare parts for decades."

Treeka considered this for a long moment.

"Don't think too long," Dr. Sylvester said, "the offer is only available for a short while."

"What are your plans, anyway? Building a cybernetic sewer patrol?" Treeka chided.

"You are correct in one respect. We are building an army, but we need help to do it. I need you, alive or in pieces, and Dr. Ash. Then no one can stop us!"

This doctor is nuts!

"What do you say, big sister? Want to have some fun blowing shit up?" Meeka said.

Treeka smiled, turned, and with lightning-fast reflexes, she removed blades that were banded against her arms and threw both at the same time. One struck Dr. Sylvester in the hand, and he dropped the shotgun. The other blade grazed Meeka's new skin. Her sister screamed and then jumped on Treeka's back like some feral cat, clawing at her face, neck, and hair. Treeka backhanded Meeka, and she went flying. The doctor dove for the smaller gun, but Treeka was faster and scooped it up and got a shot off. It hit the doctor's arm, which flopped to his side. Treeka looked at the gun's setting; the intensity level was set to the blue zone.

That setting must be some kind of stun.

Treeka heard a boom as one of the windows in the train car shattered. Small pieces of glass flew everywhere, inside and outside of the car. Some of the glass shards hit Treeka in the face. She looked to see Meeka falling on her ass from the shotgun's kickback. Meeka got up and was trying to find a way to reload the weapon but was having trouble. Treeka changed the setting on the smaller gun to the red zone. The weapon issued a high-pitched squealing sound. She spun around, looking for a target. The doctor and Meeka were regrouping, and he was helping Meeka reload the shotgun. She wanted to end him more than anything. She pointed the gun at the doctor. Her hands shook. She didn't trust herself not to hit Meeka.

I don't want to kill my sister. I've got to get that shotgun away from her somehow.

"Yes! Now die, fucker," Meeka said as she pointed the shotgun in Treeka's direction. She ran back into the train car to regroup, trying to avoid getting hit. Another blast hit the train car.

That was too close.

Treeka scrambled into the train car and began searching for an alternate, more precise weapon. The gun she had was great, but she wasn't trained in its use, and she didn't trust her aim with Meeka out there. She surveyed the train car, but only found the violent aftermath of the carnage the weapon had caused. There was another booming sound, followed by another explosion of glass and other debris. A gaping hole formed in the side of the rail car.

Then she saw it. A wardrobe was visible at the far end of the train car. She sprinted toward it as more windows shattered. Fragments of glass peppered her already damaged skin. Treeka dove toward the wardrobe. As she opened the wardrobe, a small item about the size of a tennis ball hit her. Her eyes widened as she realized what it was: a grenade. She had not seen one up close before, but she had seen plenty in movies. This one had several LEDs. She snatched it and threw it toward a blown-out window. It hit the side of the car and flew toward the opposite end of the car, which exploded. The blast was incredible. She was knocked off her feet as the wall on the far side of the train car was blown to bits. She heard maniacal laughter from Meeka.

"It's stuck!" the doctor said.

"Are you sure you're using it correctly?" Meeka said.

What in the hell are they talking about?

Treeka looked out of one of the gaping holes in the train car to see Meeka holding the shotgun over her shoulder like some kind of deranged cowgirl. The doctor had resumed his place at her side and was fiddling with something small.

I hope it's not another grenade!

Treeka took a brief pause in the action to resume her hunt for something—anything—she could use against the increasing attacks. To her surprise, the armoire was still intact. She opened it and found a suit. It seemed to be at least a size too large, but it appeared to be armored. She gave it only a cursory glance, but when she saw the scabbard, her plans changed. She dove into the wardrobe as two other windows shattered. Part of the wardrobe splintered, as well.

I wish I had my cybernetic interface.

Treeka snatched the scabbard and removed the sword. It was not just any sword, but to her astonishment, it belonged to a samurai master.

This is not just any samurai sword, this belongs to one of my father's men. I'm sure of it.

She got into the suit while Meeka was reloading. The suit felt loose, but Treeka found a button on the outside, near the collar. When she pressed it, the suit pressed against her body and formed a tight bond that felt like an extension of her skin. To her surprise, the familiar look of her cybernetic interface appeared.

System Message:

Compatible external interface found.

Cybernetic functions online.

AI functions restored.

"It's good to have you back, Treeka. I've missed you," Eliza said.

"Can you guide me out of here?" Treeka said.

"The suit that you are wearing is a prototype of an army exosuit," Eliza explained. "Although it is experimental, it can sustain damage from some physical effects."

"From a gunshot?"

"Not a direct hit, but it will deflect any fragments from indirect hits."

"That will have to do."

Treeka waited until Meeka was reloading for what seemed like the thirtieth time before making her move. She ran out of the half-demolished train car and toward the doctor. Her speed was increased with the new suit; it was like someone had given her a speed boost. Her fist landed on Dr. Sylvester's face, and she heard a satisfying snap as something crushed in his face. Moments later, Meeka hit her with something hard; Treeka realized Meeka was wielding the deadly gun like a club. The next blow was aimed at Treeka's head. She ducked, then hit Meeka in the chest. Meeka toppled back but stayed on her feet. Then she tried to use the shotgun again, but only a clicking sound emitted from the weapon.

"You fucking bitch," the doctor said.

Treeka turned to see him holding a gun that looked like a metal tube with a glass cylinder. He was close enough to kiss her. Before Treeka could react, he shoved the gun into Treeka's side and pulled the trigger. The violation of the injector caused a burning sensation, and her neck throbbed. Treeka responded by performing a roundhouse kick to his head. The doctor fell to the ground and didn't move.

How'd he sneak up on me?

Meeka jumped onto Treeka's back and started biting her ear, tearing a small piece off. Treeka felt the sensation of blood pouring down her neck and into the suit. She grabbed Meeka, then threw her toward the train car with enough force to dent it. She heard something crack, and Meeka screamed in pain. Her sister tried to get up, but one of her legs didn't work.

"I'm going to kill you, sister," Meeka said.

"Why are you following this man? He's brought nothing but pain," Treeka yelled.

"He's going to save us from the Reckoning."

Before she could ask more, Treeka heard a rush of confused voices and a stampede of people rushing toward her position. The sound of the babbling crowd seemed to be coming from everywhere at once.

System Message:

You have been injected with a drug that is attempting to affect your biological nervous system.

I think it's time to leave.

"Eliza, what the fuck is happening to me?" Treeka asked her AI.

"Analyzing . . . The doctor injected you with a neurotoxin that is attacking your nervous system. Although the suit prevented all the medicine from entering your system, you will probably start feeling its effects soon. I advise you get to a safe location immediately," Eliza said.

"Then get me the hell out of here."

"Do I have your permission to control the suit, for long enough to get you to a minimum safe distance?" Eliza asked.

Treeka's vision began to blur, and the crazy sound of whatever was charging toward her made the experience surreal.

"Yes," she said, "let's go!"

The AI guided her body through a small tunnel and up two flights of stairs. She watched her body take the steps two at a time. It was like she was a passenger in her own body.

"We are now at the street level. Ceding control of all bodily functions, please step through the door to complete your escape," Eliza said.

Treeka took a moment to catch her breath, and she looked around to get a lay of the land. She was at the end of some sort of maintenance shaft and atop a landing. A door with an Emergency Exit Only sign was close by. The only other exit was down a flight of stairs. She assumed that was the way the AI had taken her.

Need to rest for a short while.

Treeka took a step back. Her back found the wall. Her legs gave way, and as she slid down the wall, she closed her eyes to see an image of her favorite oak tree. She smiled.

Father . . . I'm coming home!

After Treeka had rested and made it out of the hellhole, she checked the suit's functions. Her power was less than ten percent and dropping. She also felt the lingering effects of the drug, and her mouth was dry. Treeka didn't know how long she'd been out, but it had been long enough for the drug to have worked its way through her body. However, she felt more lucid than she had when the AI was guiding her to the exit.

Treeka found herself on Broadway, walking aimlessly in morning rush-hour traffic. She nearly got run over by an autonomous taxi, but she was free. Then she heard a scream. Treeka stared in disbelief; people seemed to be running amok in the streets, grabbing anything they could. She saw people getting pulled out of cars and beaten by half-naked people.

Are the attackers wearing hospital gowns from the doctor's underground clinic?

Police cars were driving through the area, but none stopped to help others.

"Eliza," Treeka asked, "what happened? How long was I out?"

"You were unconscious for nine hours and fifty-three minutes. Doc Chop's legion has been unleashed. Did you notice the attackers are all wearing hospital gowns?" Eliza said.

Someone was calling Treeka's name. She looked in the direction of the voice and saw a vehicle pulling up to the curb, as well as a familiar face. The boy who had found her and Meeka—and who had tried to help her—was about three feet away. It was only days ago, but it felt like a lifetime had passed.

Nigel, that's his name! Treeka thought.

Two women and two teenaged girls were with Nigel in the car.

"Treeka, get in if you want our help," Nigel said.

She squeezed into the car. It was a tight fit, but she could get in without sitting on someone.

"What happened?" Treeka said.

"The Reckoning is upon us," the woman driving said.

"What reckoning?" Treeka asked.

"It's a long story, but the world's infrastructure is failing, and collapse is imminent," Nigel said.

"Are we leaving the city?"

"Not yet—we need to save someone first."

"Who?"

"Rick Watson, my father."

"Where are you going to find him in all of this?" Treeka said.

"I don't know yet, but he was tracking a cyborg named Nozomi to a location near here. We just have to backtrack his movements and get to the underground."

"I know where he is," Treeka said.

She dreaded going back into the underground. It was not because she feared the doctor, but she didn't think she had the strength to kill her sister.

CONTINUE THE ADVENTURE

I hope you enjoyed reading **Echoes of Silence**. I invite you to continue Treeka's adventure with **Catalyst of Pain**. The exciting follow-up to **Echoes of Silence.**

I invite you to join my reader group to learn more about this upcoming book. To sign up visit: https://cyberhunterorigins.com

Pre-Order Catalyst of Pain and it will be delivered to your eReader the moment its available.

A FAVOR

Thank you for reading my book.

Reviews are very important for an author. When I get more reviews on my books, it allows them to stay more visible. If you want to help me put out books more quickly, then please review this one.

Thank you.
D. B. Goodin

ACKNOWLEDGMENTS

Developmental & Copy Editing by Hayley Evans
Proofreading by Beth Doward
Cover Design by Konstantine Designs
Paperback Cover Design by Warren Design
Special Thanks to my advanced reader and launch teams.

ABOUT THE AUTHOR

D. B. Goodin has had a passion for writing since grade school. After publishing several nonfiction books, Mr. Goodin ventured into the craft of fiction to teach Cybersecurity concepts in a less-intimidating fashion. Mr. Goodin works as a Principal Cybersecurity Analyst for a major software company based in Silicon Valley and holds a Master's in Digital Forensic Science from Champlain College.

Cyber Hunter Origins
Synapse of Ash
Echoes of Silence
Catalyst of Pain (Fall 2021)
Silent Assassins Society (Summer 2022)

Cyber Teen Project
White Hat Black Heart
War With Black Iris
The Making of Cyber Teen Project
Reckoning of Delta Prime
Crisis At Worlds End

Cyber Overture
Sonorous
Chromatic
Resonance
Ensemble
Ramble

Interstellar Online

Blast Off

Cassidy's Fleet (Fall 2021)